Jimmy Crack Corn

ALSO BY GLENN CARLEY

Polenta at Midnight: Tales of Gusto and Enchantment in North York

Good Enough from Here

Il Vagabondo: An Urban Opera

Jimmy Crack Corn
A Novel in C Minor

Glenn Carley

Rock's Mills Press
Oakville, Ontario • Rock's Mills, Ontario
2022

Published by
Rock's Mills Press
www.rocksmillspress.com

Copyright © 2022 by Glenn Carley.
All rights reserved. Reproduction in whole or in part without the written
permission of the Publisher is strictly prohibited.

Cover photograph by Michael Angelo Molinaro.
Photograph copyright © 2022 by Michael Angelo Molinaro

Library and Archives Canada Cataloguing in Publication data has been applied for
by the Publisher.

For information, including bulk, retail and wholesale orders and permissions
requests, please contact the Publisher at customer.service@rocksmillspress.com.

For Mary,
and all those souls who protect innocence

Chord i
(my master's gone away)

"I'm 21 or so and the Old Boy dies. We plant him up at the Dug Hill Cemetery and it is just us; my brother and the Old Gal and me. We are the only ones left standing. Everybody stops coming around to see the Old Boy after his stroke and part of it is, like, his fault, because he gets kind of crabby—a real pain in the arse. Anyway, we plant him and I read something out of a book called *Heaven and Hell*. It hurt like hell so I tore the page out, threw it in the hole and it just flutters down on top of the coffin: but it isn't really a coffin, it is more like a box. Same as the Old Gal's a little later on. I remember we picked one out from the glossy funeral catalogue called the 'Eden-100'. Plywood with some green felt on it. We laugh because at least we knew where she is going, you know? Then we all come home and spend the next 24 hours sipping rye and talking—teary and all that malarkey, but it feels good to get it out. We want to make sure the Old Gal is not a mess or anything."

"My Mom was a mess after my Dad croaked. You should have seen her! It took her a while to come out of it."

"I know. The women are usually stronger than the fellas, though. But let me tell you this: Time does the *do-si-do*. A couple years pass by and for some reason I'm back in *small town Oncewuz* (that's where I grew up) and my brother is back from somewhere. (He is always on the go.) Anyway, we sit down over a smash and reminisce over the Old Boy. Out of the wild blue, don't ask me why, I want to go up to Dug Hill and pay him a visit, all sentimental-like. So, we hop in the car and go up there. We drive around and the thing is we know we planted him near an oak tree. I collect four acorns, one for each of us and the hell of it is, they are still in the ashtray of my car. I drive a Maverick. *God!* So, here we are, cruising around, nice and slow: We I.D. the tree, park the car and get out. Twenty minutes later, dammit all to hell, we still cannot find him. *And the other Jimmy Crack Corn.* I tell you, we are pissed!"

"Didn't you buy a headstone or anything?"

"No. We should have though, because it hurt the hell out of us. All we put in were those *jeezis* 6-by-6-inch marble squares with his name on it. Not even the date. That's right, corner markers I think they call them. What did we know about death? Make it all up as we go along:

'*Going live*', we call it. We figure the markers will be enough. What we don't figure on, is that he is buried on a slope and the run-off from the rain, covers everything in mud-just like a finger-painting or something. The point is we are pissed right out of our minds. We don't tell the Old Girl and then, you know, leave and never do a thing about it."

"It's *definitely tough being an orphan.*"

"It is. Thanks, but wait till I tell you. A couple years later, after the Old Girl leaves *Oncewuz*, she settles in and then dies. This time we figure we'll plant her right. There is a plot with her mom and dad already, you know, sleeping there, with room for her and her baby brother, my Uncle; but that's another story. Do not get me started on that! Once again, we go 'micro' on the funeral, as far as people go. Just me and my wife, my brother, her brother, two cousins, the kids and a minister. The minister I know from my church days. We went to school together, but I'm not that church-y, you know? Never took to it. For some reason I hate collectives for the greater good. I don't like being forced to think the same as everyone else. Don't get me wrong, I don't mind what they do: just don't git in on me, right? I figure I'm more spiritual, than religious and that's just the way it is. So, like I say, this time we get it right. A head stone for her that says: '*wife of the Old Boy, buried in Oncewuz*' and on his, it says: '*husband of the Old Girl, buried in Neverwuz*'. There are hummingbirds on both of them, because she likes hummingbirds and it looks sweet. We are glad to get it done. There is a funny jingle with the funeral home that the Old Gal sings. We get a kick out of it.

"Ashes to ashes, dust to dust, if Rotz don't git you, Nettel must!"

"*That's a knee slapper! Smoke?*"

"Thanks. Let me buy you another drink. You take it straight up like me. You don't take mix, right?"

"*That's right. I am allergic to pop for some reason.*"

"But listen, it doesn't end here. A couple years pass and for whatever reason, I don't go back to Dug Hill to see if they do the job right. So, I phone up my brother and tell him I am going to go and check the Old Boy out. He's on the other side of the planet now, and I never see him ... which is a pain in the ass, because we're like, really close, you know?"

"*... and the other I-don't-care, right?*"

"Right. So, here it is: I make the trip, go back to Dug Hill, spot the oak tree and *Bingo!* The headstone looks beautiful. I don't need to spend a lot of time there, because I get sad, see, so I search around for four more acorns. All the tops busted off the ones in my ashtray and I lost one. So there are only three left. I gather four ripe ones, with the caps still on, nice and green. For some reason I get down and feel *blue*. When I am a kid, I sit on the Old Boy's lap and watch television with him. He lets me twirl his wedding ring around while we watch the *idiot box*. I get this idea to pry one of the corner stones out of the ground and take it home with me—maybe put it in the garden—I don't know, just to keep the Old Boy with me a little bit. Weird, eh? I don't ever want to search again and not find him. To hell with that. I actually dig the corner stone out. Takes me half an hour, too, because I use my hands and a stick to try to force it. I find a twig to dig the mud out of the letters of his name. Finally, I yank it out, toss the square in a green plastic garbage bag I keep in the trunk and go home. I leave it in the car for days and then fish it out and put it in the backyard. Every time I am in the garden his name glares up at me and I get the creeps. Payback, I guess. I probably should have left it, is the guilty way to tell it. So, I park it upside down, out of the way, in a corner of my barn. The other day, I walk by it and Christ, somebody turns it right side up! Shoot me in the heart or what? Like I really need a reminder to accuse me that I am lost. I realize now that I have to get rid of it. But the thing is I don't know how to get rid of it. I think, *'maybe I'll get a chisel and chop it up and chuck it out'*, but I might not mess it up enough. It will be like those pill bottles: if you throw one out with your name on it, everybody knows what drugs you take. *'Ok, I will drive up to the River of Joy, where he likes to fish and throw it in there,'* I tell myself; but then I go, *'Right, some kid will find it lure diving, call the cops and they'll trace it back to me, easy peasy.'* I have no idea what to do.

"OK fellas, it's getting near closing time. Anything else?"

"Why don't you go back to Dug Hill and put it back in the ground?"

"I think about that all the time. Maybe I will. Can you spare another smoke before you leave? If you don't play a sport, be one!

"Sure. Listen. Have a nice night, and if you can't have a nice night, don't mess it up for anyone else. I'll see you around."

I awake in spirit-form. There is a piano in my head and I hear chords.
It is an odd thing about loss. It leaves a space I am desperate to fill.
There is no rest when the notes come and when they come, they
form melodies in my mind. I know there is a song there, somewhere,
but it never plays itself out, until I get up off my arse and do something. A call and response to random action.

I beat the sun by an hour and make time to boil an instant coffee to swish out the noise. I intend to leave before rush hour, drive
down an octave or two to the highway, and head east to *Oncewuz*.
It is a good morning. The chilly air is a refreshing reprieve from the
heat that comes. I finish my coffee, catch a quick shave, pack a small
cooler and get out the door as the edge of the horizon mixes her pink
with glorious blue. I put the visor down in a feeble attempt to control
the sun.

Of course, trucks are everywhere, like schools of carp, and I am
foolish to think I can beat rush hour in this city. I fight the frustration
and settle in. I listen to the smooth thrum of the motor, see that my
tank is full and re-adjust both mirrors. Everything is behind me now.
The sensation of leaving is like a skittery horse who kicks at the top
rails, frothing to escape. Suddenly, I break free and run to the mesa
as fast as my haunches take me. Motion overrides thought. There is
no space and time then, no boundary, no cause and effect, no mea-
surement between fixed points. I find my inner grin and when I get
the inner grin, all music becomes colour. The colour reminds me of
finger paintings. This notion of pictures becoming, unbecoming and
re-becoming, equally capable of smearing back to nothing, at the tip
of my finger. It is nice to take control.

I come to at the edge of an inside joke. *"The Place of Four Fingers"*
is a set of four high rises, spaced like digits that stretch to scratch the
skyline. The Old Boy's baby sister lives in the middle finger, twenty
third floor. Ida Orchard and Mister Ted. Orchard is a family name.
She is my favourite. I call her Auntie Peach Pit and she calls me "LP",
short for "Little Pest." There is no way I feel shy around Auntie Peach
Pit. She does not let me. It is not like she is full of herself. She is full of
everything and cannot wait to tell everyone about it. I talk about cra-

zy things around her. Things I never have an opinion on. She makes me feel good.

I forget the reason they introduce Uncle Ted to me as Mister Ted, but his moniker sticks to both of us. He addresses me as Mister back. I feel grown-up and respected; like a kid actually matters in the company of an adult. Later, when I learn to observe, I find out Auntie Peach Pit is smacked around by her ex-husband. He is a grease-monkey. I hear he has polio and drinks like a fish. I want to pull his lungs out. Everybody thinks Mister Ted is a much better catch. He lost his left thumb above the first joint. A derrick severed it and he is not afraid to show it off or let us feel the rounded bone underneath. He is a hunter and has a pile of *Argosy* magazines with stories like *"How I survived a bear mauling"* and *"Landing the monster Muskie."* Auntie Peach Pit and Mister Ted don't have children together, so he never thinks to stash his other magazines. To be honest, it is no big deal. The wild look in an elk's eye holds my attention. It thrashes when an arrow pierces it. Hunters carve it up in the field. I look straight down into a Big Mouth bass's lung. A shiny lure pierces its lip. I watch it rocket up out of the weeds and twist in the wind. Inevitably, I am bored to tears in the high rise. I gob off the balcony till my spit runs dry, or go next door to a different lobby. I press every orange button in the elevator and run away. I am desperate to drive back east to *Oncewuz* and gallop with my friends.

The Place of Four Fingers slips past me now. The highway trims down to two lanes and the blue expanse of the lake opens up to make the view magnificent again. I smell the rich scent of tree-breath, so luscious and green, it teams with cicadas and peepers. They sleep in cool shadows, to hide from the sun. A yellow-tail hawk perpetually twists in a languid sky. He carves the air with a malevolent power, to watch with indifference and smug satisfaction. He will never go hungry over the field. The wheat is golden; the oats, warm-amber, like honey. The corn is so sexy. It grows everywhere. Fenced along the highway, the stalks wash back like emerald waves that surge over hills between island clusters of oak and maple. I never listen to the radio when I drive. There is too much going on. I intentionally keep my mind unfettered so my spirit may witness the harmonics of colour.

Within the colours, I remember a man with one arm. He drives a standard. Two boys hitchhike and I see him pull over to pick them up. The boys break free from the confines of *Oncewuz* to return home after the thrill of the hunt. A hitch to the next town intoxicates, for no other reason than to grow up and run wild. I ride shotgun and wonder how-the-hell this one-arm codger shifts gears. Each time the engine revs, he puts the clutch in, takes his hand off the wheel, reaches across his chest and moves the stick-shift. The car veers to the right then, catches the shoulder but somehow jerks back onto the tarmac. We ask politely to be let off early and walk the long way home. It is a relief to satisfy our grown-up quotient; like a tick on a bubble-gum card checklist, we collect enough experience for one day. I wonder how he drives like that and still manages to smoke. I try it myself to see how it is done.

Dat-dat and *datly-dat* on the snare drum of memory. The staccato tap of my fingers upon the steering wheel returns my attention to the highway. The road is smooth. I spot a service centre up ahead and feel the urge. I slow the car, pull off, follow the arrows and park. After I *squirt my pickle*, I buy some *go-juice*, a bottle of water and a pop. The cooler is long empty and my *egg sammi* is gone. My *townie dialect* returns, the closer I get to *Oncewuz*. Elvis calls milk *"butch,"* and I fight the urge to tell the waitress not to put butch in my *bean*. Like a pitstop at the Indy 500 I am sufficiently suffonsified, good-to-go and urgent to fly. The acceleration lane pulls my car up to speed.

It is pines by the road now. Tall ones with the shivers. When I whiz by Sleepy-ville, I spy a giant Apple with a door in it. People buy pies. It is a landmark. Up ahead and under a bridge, I observe a man set down his pack. He adjusts his pants and makes ready to stick out his thumb. I know the look. Perhaps, I am nostalgic for adventure. I decrease speed and pull over onto the gravel apron. I eyeball the man in the rear-view mirror and as the dust clears from the road, I lean over to roll down the passenger side window.

"Where you headed, chum?"

"I could use a ride to *Oncewuz*, bud. You going that way?"

"You know what? I come from there. Hop in."

I take my hand off the wheel to signal. The car picks up speed on the crunch of gravel, shimmies to get lane-ward, roars and then settles in.

My travelling companion introduces himself as "Fizzy Jack." This spooks me, because I know a Fizzy Jack, in *Oncewuz*. How many Fizzy Jacks can there be? The Fizzy Jack I know scares the hell out of me. Hell, he scares the hell out of all of us. This is because he is quirky. When kids give him a pop, they stand back and watch him drink it in one go. Fizzy gets the palsy, then like he is allergic or something. He jerks and jack-hammers and yells out *"Buh dee chee chee, Buh dee chee chee"* for some unknown reason. It is not like he is nuts. He is an unlucky 'runt-kid', filled with gristle and string and knobbly at the knee. He is destined to be invisible to girls. Nothing surrounded by nothing equals nothing is the sad calculus of him. He knows it too: too many pimples and always the jitter-bug thing. Some of us feel sorry for him and share our chips, or later on, a smoke, but half the town takes a piss out of Fizzy and he knows that too. I have three friends and they know ten other guys that mock him so perfectly, it is award-winning. You have to laugh and I guess when I feel like it, I can *"Buh dee chee chee"* with the best of them. It's not like I do it everyday and most days, it does not feel like I am cruel. I am just too stupid to know, too gorged on belonging and acceptance to get hungry. Most of us never go hungry a day in our lives. I can tell Fizzy Jack is always hungry. Time and again, he comes back for more.

I offer him a water. He asks me if I have a pop.

"Are you sure?" I say.

He cracks it and drinks most of it down in one go. I cringe because I know what is coming. When he goes *"Buh dee chee chee," "Buh dee chee chee,"* we both guffaw our heads off. In an eye blink, we are pals. I suppose we know each other in the empathy of our being. We always have. Somehow, do not ask me why, we are soul mates.

He is in spirit-form, like me, I think to myself.

Bedazzled by the sun as it streams through the windshield, I behold Fizzy Jack split into four people. There are three friends with him. Substance and form transform meaning, even gain possibility when gravity is gone. My memories replace the linear notion of time and how it ticks. Like I say, the removal of all reference points makes space irrelevant, too. Distance is measured only by the hot and cold of desire and affection. I navigate through my heart and lungs now. Perception and no guessing. My strange font of love and maybe, wisdom is the crazy way to tell it. Fizzy Jack just gets it.

I know The Dummy before he introduces himself. I know Bumbo and Clarence the Cross-Eyed Lion, that way, too. They all chat in the backseat of my car, like there is no tomorrow. They roll the windows down. The breeze engulfs us and we drink the drink of giddiness. I take a slug of water. Fizzy slam-dunks the remainder of his pop and wipes his mouth across his skinny forearm. He is such a tooth pick. *"Buh dee chee chee!"* we all laugh.

"In the days before apps," he testifies, "when boys walked the earth, we spent every second on a Saturday morning in our quest for empty pop bottles."

"Five cents for the big bottles, two cents for the munchkin ones!" Bumbo pipes in.

"That's right!" Fizzy continues. "Get it down to a science: comb each hedge, check all fifty-gallon garbage drums and look in every ditch. In zero time you find enough dough to march back to Dummy's, count the bottles like soldiers, sound off, divide and conquer. There is a variety store on every corner with metal bike racks to crack popsicles on. Are we rich or what?"

"Do you remember those pops with the cork liners?" I ask.

Clarence the Cross-Eyed Lion remembers. "I got three ginger ales in a row that way. Old Mrs. Phil just laughs, rolls her eyes and points to the cooler. She is sweet to me and doesn't care which way my eyes roll. I love that."

"Tell me how you lost your voice again?" I ask The Dummy.

"My vocal chords didn't really get born right," he says.

"Well, the rest of you did," Fizzy states as a matter of fact.

It is a good enough explanation as any and we all nod.

"We hereby knight you Marcel Marceau from this day forth," I say for all of us. Release me from being mean.

"Once, in grade six, my best friend nominates me for *Mister Fun Fair*," I confess. "My brother makes a couple of campaign posters. He feels sorry for me. Of the 600 kids in the school, I lose the election by a landslide. My best friend does not even vote for me. I am too stupid to get mad.

"At least I have 79 more friends on record then you, arsehole!" I tell him.

"I voted for you," Bumbo says.

Fizzy looks over the back seat. "I love that you voted, even though they all call you a retard."

"Do you know this guy makes more money on the milk wagon than all of us put together?" Marcel points out.

"You come by our house every week," I tell them. "Like clockwork. Horse stops. You jump off the wagon with a full six-pack of milk quarts. Run up to the porch. Plop them down. Pick up the empties and race to the back of the wagon and hop back on. I watch you from the screen but I am too scared to come out and talk to you.

"Everyone is," Bumbo says, as a matter of fact.

"Did you get my chocolate bar," I say, "I left it for you on top of the empties."

"I did," Bumbo replies. "I don't like that kind so I gave it to Old Gray. That is why he took a dump on the road in front of your house."

We talk like this for a while and get it out of our system. Suddenly, green highway signs appear. They breeze by quickly to announce the early approach to *Oncewuz*. Fizzy says something curious. "We are not driving on the road, we are more like ideas propelled in a bloodstream," he tells us.

There are two gateways into *Oncewuz*. The decision decides by its own accord to exit at the first turnoff. It is impossible for me to change course. All motion slows, the car yaws around the bend and we come to a stop at a 'T-junction' this side of the River of Joy. We are above the first damn of that great, wet, flowing truth, slightly north of Dug Hill. There are no cars behind me and I hesitate.

Fizzy reads my mind: "You are not ready to go yet, are you?"

Bumbo answers for me. "Not sure why you come in the first place."

Marcel breaks the impasse. "Let's go up to Stinkford!" he says.

The car turns left. The River of Joy flows proud with its chest out, so majestically on the right. It is a beautiful lazy time in the afternoon, when the texture of water dazzles with wavelets and each baby-wave takes its full measure of the sun. The tiny waves throw off laser winks. Flickering induces slumber and I look away for fear I may grow blind.

I did go blind once for a day or two. Saturday afternoon job at the stereo store subbing in for Fizzy. I am up on the roof holding a steel mesh while the hired-hand welds it to a square of angle iron. I have no gloves. He tells me not to look, but the sparks burn my *geezis* arms, so of course I look. About a hundred times. I get a couple bucks for the work, go home and that night, the inside of my eyeballs are scratched out, like static on the television before the stations open at sunrise. Our neighbour tells the Old Boy to do something about it. Burn his arse! By Tuesday, my eyes are back to normal, so my father lets it go. Nobody sues anybody in those days.

The road leads us north, past a mixture of scrub bush and ancient gnarled trees that lean out over the water at intervals. Their deep shadows mute the dappled light. Citizens on lawn chairs, lean forward to inspect open tackle boxes. Each box, stair-steps to display a proud array of red, white and sea-green lures, sharp and fishy. All the monofilament lines are cast and bob nervously with nets close by. This is my favourite part of the great river, when all time stands still. Piano chords resound and nothing matters. Not far from this sacred tableau, the road curves and a shoe factory appears. It is the sign that The Rope is nearby. Before you go to The Rope, there is a place on the left for kids to pull off and dump their bikes. The jumble is so careless it is plain to see why kickstands are obsolete. This cavalier gesture by boys is a magnet for constant lectures when observed. An overgrown path is visible for those in the know. The scent of milkweed, vetch and goldenrod give it away. Cicadas whine loudly in the dry heat, out of sight but everywhere. I often wonder how they remain hidden when the air surrounds us in song.

A shade offers coolness. A small gurgle of stream, slips over rocks to complement the effect. Dense green clots of watercress wait to be picked and *shnibbled*. The water is cold to the touch. Up over the ridge, the trail grows hard with stones half-emerged from the runoff. In the trick of an epoch, *Boo Boo's Erratic* looms before us framed by the woods. It is a little farther than I remember it to be. This wonderful boulder, big-as-a-house, left stubbornly behind, when glaciers get their slow-legs and retreat. Worn smooth and irregular in places, its cave-like recess is charred black by thousands of bush parties and the spoor paintings of drunken souls. We climb to the top if we want to and we always, frankly, have to. It is our rite of passage; a way to boost our self esteem, alone or together with the pack. Simple days in our glacial acquisition of competence and freedom.

Not a single teacher in any grade, in any school, possesses the common sense to tell us it is famous. So, we take their lesson plan, all Huck Finn, into our own hands and tell *them* about the boulder, big-as-a-house up near Stinkford.

"Oh yes, Boo Boo's Erratic," they say with a dismissive distraction that rankles our scorn.

Marcel sticks his hand up. "Do you know what wild watercress tastes like?" he boasts. We love him for it.

This being said and remembered, Fizzy calls me out of my trance. We climb down, slide the last six feet and drop to the ground. I gather up my companions and we return to the road.

The crazy tangle of bikes, separates and morphs into a car. The car signals. It lets a fellow pass and I pull onto the highway in hot pursuit.

A thousand yards up, around a bend defined by the river, our excitement is palpable. I pull off the road just past The Rope. We all have our bathing suits on. The towels around our necks now drape carelessly on bush-tops as we race to the tree. It is an old willow of course, massive, with bark so furrowed you can sink most of your fingertips into the corky ruts. The tree does what all riverside willows must do. It defies gravity, bursts into the sky and sends cascades of leaves in spray after spray over the water. There is an unruly limb, sturdy as a telephone pole that reaches twenty feet over the water. The laws of gravity threaten to snap it. In the days before apps, when boys walk the earth, some unknown genius shimmies out to the end and loops a thick nautical rope around the limb. The bark at this point is worn smooth like the rind of a wedding ring. 'Till death do us part' and we vow our timeless pledge to have fun.

Ashes to ashes, dust to dust if Rotz don't git you, Nettel must.

The trunk of the willow twists skyward at a crazy angle with hand and foot holds worn in wonderfully. We all look like *Mowgli* when we scamper up the bark. The motion is primordial and I always pause to observe it. At the highest point we can climb, an ancient limb sculpts down to a nub. There is room to place one good foot on it. The other foot stands on top of the instep. It is difficult to stand that way for too long. I hug the girth of the trunk for dear life, take my turn and wait. Wet bark has no smell. It is rough on the cheek. A soul in the water grabs the lower knot and pumps the rope for distance. It snaps treeward to catcalls when I miss it the first time. In the school of hard knocks, the thick knot on the end of the rope that acts as a mercy seat, brains every one of us, at least once.

"And twice on Sundays," Bumbo says.

The fun begins. The first thousand times, we Tarzan over the water to freefall from maximum loft. Inevitably, the 'hogging' starts. An ape rides the rope over the water, back to the trunk, over the water and back to the trunk. He is careful not to bash his knees. Finally, he lets go. We hate him when he falls and forgive him when he surfaces. In the law of pay-backs, turn begets turn begets turn.

In due time, the experiments begin. It is necessary to see how many primordial boys can swing out over the River en masse. The lifetime record is six, not including the apes who hurtle, miss and plummet to their deaths in the water below. Pity the chimp on the bottom whose inner thighs burn from the pressure of the mercy seat. War hoops and a serpentine mass of legs, knees and arms, foam and bubbles, drive all laughter to the bottom of the River of Joy, only to bob up at random intervals to try for the record again.

Fizzy, Mister Marceau, Clarence, Bumbo and I get our turn. The droplets tingle when the air meets our skin when we stumble onto the shore. We eat peanut butter sandwiches while the sun dries us off. Before we leave, we are careful to put towels down on the car seats and get as much sand off our feet as we can.

The road takes us north another five minutes. We turn right over a black bridge that spans the river and pull into the solitary gas station in the heart of Stinkford.

Stinkford's claim to fame is her black bear. She starts out as a cub. Despite the odds, she grows bigger and blacker. Her home is a concrete pad, encased by iron bars with a metal lid on the top. Three-quarters of this makeshift zoo catches the full brunt of the sun and the sun pins most of the bear down most of the day. Her hair is matted. The heat cooks off the stink of her feces in a way blue tail flies just love. So many blue tail flies and she is just too sun-addled or bored out of her gourd to stop panting, pull her tongue in and close her mouth. There is a rope outside of the bars to keep us zoo-goers back far enough so our fingers won't be chomped. Bumbo comforts her—we all do—when ever we venture that far north along the River of Joy. He slops water on the bear's mouth. Some of it gets on her nose and she sneezes. It is not clear if the owners make money off her because the store is a dump. The bear has no name and there is no charge to gawk. It is the only place in Stinkford to get gas and cigarettes; so yes, stretch your legs and go have a smoke over by the bear. After a time, I grow stupid looking at her and I decide it is time to leave.

"I will drive into *Oncewuz* along the far side of the river," I announce to no one in particular.

"We will stay with the bear," Fizzy Jack, Marcel Marceau and Bumbo reply.

"I'll ride with you," Clarence the Cross-Eyed Lion volunteers.

The ride south is surreal. There is no vertigo, yet the black curves of tarmac seem to separate themselves from the white lines which run against the momentum. Sumaches turn red and a breeze creates tiny licks of fire, slightly out of view. Giant reeds, hairy on top bend languidly in a motion made aqueous by the air. The wind-buffet of a tanker truck bursts upon the car, makes it shudder and roll thru slipstreams until it settles into place.

Clarence the Cross-Eyed Lion points and I reduce speed. We turn right down a pot-holed laneway that runs parallel to the scrub, trees and shale that border the River of Joy. A snapping turtle defiantly stares us down from the middle of the lane. We do our utmost not to squish it like a pancake. Clarence turns back to look all wall-eyed through the window. When the dust clears, he slumps in his seat and calls me an asshole. I do not try to kill it.

Pothole gives way to sand and sand leads to a gravel apron that defines a small parking lot. There are no other cars. The air smells of fish and whiffs of gasoline from the boats rocking down below in the lock. *Evenrude* engines growl in neutral to create a wallowing suck-sound that reverberates off the high cement walls. The air is damp with excitement as the water level resurrects three bobbing boats to the upper level of our River. The lockmaster looks sharp in his crisp tan uniform. He nods. When it is time, he corkscrews his finger and Clarence and I grab the long handles of the lock key. We walk counter clockwise to open the gates. There is a hem of green grass by the pier and after, we sit in the sun to rest. We violate the townie 'shithawks' by our presence. They angrily screech over head, or indignantly awk awk awk with silly tip-toe steps along the pier. We mock them and then worry they will crap on our hair. Their white and black goo is everywhere.

Bosom-y first mates untie the soaked ropes. They will soon mix an afternoon cocktail for their captains.

"I say, I'll take one of those," Clarence says jauntily. I am not sure if he is talking about a drink.

"Let's go down to the Filbert later," I laugh. "You can have a cocktail there."

The boats waddle on in a restrained procession. We wave and enjoy the names painted on the sterns: 'She got the car,' and 'No turning back', or 'What's your excuse?' Our lips curl then: "Eat shit and die," we christen the three of them. I munch on some watermelon and throw out the rinds before the ants invade. Time to pack up and head south.

The road takes us over the highway and I look for Billy's Auto Wreckers and especially Billy the Grease Monkey. Of course, he is an eye sore as much as his yard. It is defined by bent corrugated steel a mile high. Car carcasses peak over the top and there are freaking pools of motor oil, everywhere. Billy is no different and his striped railroad coveralls are always dirty at the bum. The odds are high that he either rolls a cigarette or lights one. His iconic oil-besotted five-o'clock shadow makes me feel home in a townie kind of way. It is fun to anticipate the old bastard. The first ambassador I look for when I roll in to town. Clarence likes him too.

To the left, what can I say? 'It is not pretty but it is mine.' There is a porcelain factory where they make toilet seats next to a steel factory where they make everything. Countless corrugated brown boxes give the entire side of the street a cracked Naugahyde effect; especially in a merciless sun. The rays illuminate every weed, every oil drum and every pile of tangled trash like a spotlight. A cicada will not be caught dead singing here. Snapping turtles migrate north in disgust along small, dusty laneways to the River.

"Welcome home ... *Oncewuz!*" I cry.

The River of Joy changes names at this exact point, where frothy phosphate suds puff, billow and metastasize over the shale in the shallows. It is here the carp run freely, like lewd-lipped monsters who suck up sludge along the bottom. I never see a carp I like. It is all I can do, not to pick up a ballpeen hammer and smash their ugly pusses, just to put myself out of my own misery. Even Bumbo hates carp, which says a lot because Bumbo does not hate anything.

Clarence and I turn right off the main drag. The road feels like a crossword puzzle: fifteen no-big-deal houses down, two streets across, one factory below, until the pattern takes us lower to deposit us as an afterthought at the Water Treatment plant. The parking lot is deserted. Our car lurches like we are on safari until it comes to a stop. The dust settles. A narrow pathway shunts us downward at a slight angle, past the remnants of a lost apple orchard, strewn with concrete slabs and bramble. We hear the water then and when the wind shifts, we feel its moist breath on our cheeks. Each arrival is like the first and we behold an exact moment of majesty from our footing on the east side.

The transformation of the River of Joy is ruthless. Before our eyes and before our ears the quiet dapples of wavelets or the gentle groan of rope on willow limb mutates into a fierce torrent. It snarls through precisely spaced gates, restrains itself for a moment, perhaps surprised by its own force, then releases to maul the rocks down river. It tuckers out far below the bend. It is the Purdy River now at the lock, where the power of the current is held at the will and whimsy of man. It depends on how many timbers they winch off the top. Some days the river is docile and some days it has an indifferent malevolence. On any day it cares less whether it kills you or lets you swim in it.

Clarence and I turn to look at each other and grin. *"Purdy scary, Purdy dangerous and Purdy much fun!"* we laugh in unison.

Today, perched on the east bank, the river indeed is ready to kill anything stupid enough to jump in. Fortunately, we lack judgement.

A fence of steel cable threads along the top. We climb through its sinew and get right down to stand on one of the cement ribs of the lock. Fishermen do it all the time. Three of them are out already.

They efficiently tie jigs and cast line. The monofilament has a purple hue and glints in the sun.

In the days before apps, when boys walk the earth, you almost hate to jig a carp. They are monsters, with sharp scales as hard as oyster shells and they hurt. It is so much work to get one in. Purdy damn hard to haul one up the concrete abutment without snapping the line. The method that works may take over an hour. Let the line spool out, somehow hold the rod with one hand, climb up to the top level, crawl through the cable, switch hands to get the rod through, then hold it high over your head, while the line is taught, and bends the rod into a fishhook. Walk along the pier, careful not to decapitate any one watching. Go over to the west bank, slide down the incline on your bum to stand along the wet limestone flats. Maybe get lucky enough to haul one in across a river bed, strewn with natural rock and busted slabs of concrete. And then what? You get the ugly thing in and who wants to eat it? We regard them as vermin, hate them with a passion and leave them to gasp in shallow pools, afloat in phosphate suds. Suck that, stupid.

"I never thought twice about it," Clarence the Cross-eyed Lion says.

"Me neither."

The mist is high in the middle of the river. We stand on the steel cable and bounce like apes. Only a thin line holds us back from the froth below. In the carefree innocence of youth, we ward off the possibility of death when our stomachs rise to our throats. A semblance of common-sense listens to instinct.

The mist clears. Hundreds of summer boys bounce on the cable beside us. Some run across the pier to the far shore, slip down the cut-away part on their bums to slide across the shale at water level. We know the night before that something will happen the next day. We are just never sure what it is going to be. It does not matter. Choice is a pure speculation based on the sun, for She decides if we play outdoors or in. It takes a second to know. We share a constant desire and care less if it rains. There is no set time to meet. We assemble in dribs and drabs and after a series of breakfasts we are all forced to eat.

The bicycles are hand-me-downs, but they work. We set off, always on the sidewalk, glance behind to cut to the street and ride in a knot, like horses, wild and skittery. Entitled by youth, we block the road until the first honks herd us all single-file to the edge. Main street becomes side street and side street becomes drag strip. It is all war-whoop, flat-out, all-out. There is literally no tomorrow when all of today is laughter and daring: the happy bragging rights of victory: the warm pleasure of good-natured mockery between friends.

We never use kickstands. Like I say, we lay our bikes out in the dirt and care less. We grab our towels and eagerly take in the full might of the river. The water gallops high in anger, roars along the spillway, then rears upon its haunches, before the drop. It is all frenzy and froth, current and spray. We grow quiet then; like it is church or something. We do not know why. Everything is out of control: the sound, the mist, the wet mountains of tumble, the gravity and we love it. All of us love it like Brothers. We love it yesterday, today and tomorrow. It is just life. It is just our life. A life of days that never end; days that grow dark when the street lights come on; days that wait for the sun to come back whenever the rain decides to go. Time does not matter. None of us worry about a thing. It is our privilege to live on pop and chips and when the pop and chips run out, it is our privilege to roam for empty bottles and cash them in. In the days before apps when boys walk the earth, the world is free this and free that. There is enough for everyone all the time. We just expect our bounty within the constant amusement that friendship brings.

"It wasn't like that for me and Fizzy," Clarence says to me, out of the blue.

"I know." What else can I say?

"Was it you or some other asshole that nailed me in the eye? It was outside of the snowball area too, when I wasn't looking. Was it you or some other asshole that cut open the Schaefer's ink cartridge, poured it over the snow and nailed me in the back? Did you know the ink screwed my coat? Did you know my Mom smacked me?"

"Some other asshole got you in the eye but it was me that screwed your coat," I confess.

"And can we drop the cross-eye part?"

"Yes, I say"

"... and the other *Jimmy Crack Corn and I don't care*," Clarence the Lion sings.

The towels go up on the bank, on top of the bushes to keep them dry. The water is not too violent at the first pier. Most of us hop-step over the seaweed, grasp the far wall and slip around the end to the second pier where the water roars. There is a time when you know not to do something but you do it anyway and when you do it the first time and it is fun, you have to keep doing it because you don't want to stop. You don't want anyone to stop. It is fun to watch everyone do the same thing.

Around the second pier more of the timbers are out and the water cascade is at eye level. The first shivers come. It is my turn to jump and await the possession. I howl at the sky to gather courage. It is an ancient battle cry and helps. I keep my knees high to avoid the sweep of current and get right into the frothy middle. At that moment my feet are brutally swept out from under me.

I feel the slick seaweed rush along my butt and I look straight into the mouth of the lion. Raging, out of control, the lion completely eats me, caterwauls me, tickles me with a thousand bubbles, bashes me with force. All sound is a mile away. I need to let go then, let it swallow me and if I don't fight dying, the lion spits me out coughing thirty feet down. I am out of its grip then, exhausted and I collapse in the indifferent reprieve of the shallows. It is here I get a footing, rise up, look back, howl and watch all of us, all the time, do the exact same thing, together.

We do everything we shouldn't; everything we are told not to do; ignore every lesson from school and from parents; even grow indignant at the betrayal of older brothers who go turncoat and spout warnings. Life ends when the lion swallows and does not let one of us go. I still remember the ambulance. How we all mill around and feel sick to our stomach. Nobody thinks to pick his shitty bike up out of the dirt. I hear his father comes back to get it.

"Let's blast," I say to Clarence the Pissed-Off Lion.

We pick our way back, past the knot of bikes and hop into the car. It is time to head over to Eldorado, our Street of Gold.

Clarence glances at the ashtray.

"You are missing an acorn," he says.

"I know."

"Are you going up to Dug Hill?"

"Sometime," I say.

Thankfully, we are on the far side of the Purdy and its violence acts as a barrier to any decision to go to the cemetery.

We pick our way through the outskirts, find the main drag and head into the throb of the place. The variety stores out here in the boonies are foreign. The proprietors are strange; nothing is where it should be; the candy is different; the shops smell funny. The reek of grown-ups, we like to say. I keep my guard up in an alien space and I don't enjoy it.

We make a left turn. A memory pushes me forward. It buffets me in unsteady little trots. Clarence grows chatty. He wants to tell me about Fizzy and by telling me about Fizzy, he tells me about Bumbo. By telling me about Bumbo, he tells me about Marcel. I see a lesson coming.

"Fizzy brought the temple down right on top of him," Clarence muses.

"What temple?"

"The Sampson one."

"How did he do that?" I ask.

"There is a time", Clarence the Lion says, "when it is all good for Fizzy. Nobody cares that he is jerky. At first, when the mocking comes, he goes with it, gets some laughs but then he grows to hate it. Really hate it. There is not a boy left that he can walk the earth with. He feels chained to those marble columns with the grooves in them- the ones we colour at school. His arms are spread-eagle and the rabble before him drink pop and dance the St. Vitus dance around a roaring fire. The light changes, the fire splits the night and even the shadows mock with palsy. That's how it looks to Fizzy, but Bumbo, of all people, gives him the basic math on it." He has lots of experience.

"*When ever somebody puckers up their lips and drools water down their t-shirt and all that, I first think it is the entire world. Then I realize it boils down to maybe six guys who are retarded. I can handle six guys. Pull the temple down, Fizzy!*"

"His master's gone a-way," I say to complete the tale.

We turn right and the entire street is paved comic-book yellow. I look for Donald Duck and Uncle Scrooge. We see Fizzy, Marcel and Bumbo right where the road crests. From a distance they appear as one. As we draw closer, we are able to see each of them distinctly. The warmth between them warms me. Each of them has a popsicle. Fizzy likes the blue ones, Marcel, the yellow banana one and Bumbo prefers the lemon-white for some reason. Clarence is eager to join them, so I pull over, and park in Phil's Market over by the hedge.

"*Buh dee chee chee!*"

"We got sick of the bear and hitched down from Stinkford," Fizzy says by way of explanation. "We will meet you at the Park!"

Satisfied to be back home, I stand with my hands on my hips. I hear my piano change chords. I look up and look down to take my neighbourhood in. It changes form constantly, smears some might say, so that no one image stays fixed when my gaze returns to it. Only Phil's Market does not swirl out in blues and yellows, reds and purples. I see the whorls of my fingerprints, all the way down the block, around the bend and into the small afterthought of a parking space that frames *The Handy Dandy*. The *Dandy* is the other variety store, that holds the block in place like bookends that do not match. Suddenly, with not a care in the world, I start to run. A ball heads for the road. I chase it and trip face down into a pruned-off hedge. In the pause before tears, that moment of awe that shock brings, I put my hand to my cheek and carefully peel it off. I see my complete palm print then, like a design etched on a linoleum tile. The lifeline is so fragile. My fortune is told in a moment and I am frightened to imagine the depth of the puncture. Reflexively, I wipe the bloody mess across my chest and destroy my favourite t-shirt. The boys take me inside to clean up and when I daub my cheek with toilet paper, the wound is the size of a pin-prick.

"Jimmy, you bastard. You are a Bleeder!" they laugh. (Thankfully, there are less than six apes, so I can handle it.) It is the day I get my name-tattoo in *Oncewuz*.

Bleeder begat Buzzy Buzzy begat Pinky. Pinky begat Mouse Mouse begat Squeak, Squeak begat Beamish and we all love Joel-the-Hole. There are six of us, not counting me. When boys walk the earth, we are named, indelibly. We love indelibly. There is literally no need for ink. Indelibly we age and gray, some of us die but we never lose the birth right of pals in *Oncewuz*. Nicknames do not come off, is the townie way to tell it. They can be modified but it is difficult.

The centre of the cosmos in *Oncewuz* is actually defined by three corner stores. Three swirling nebulae, each one distinct but together, they form a whole in the cosmic expanse. All reference points, on bike, on foot, later by car are taken from a strip of golden territory about eight hundred metres long, give or take. Shoot an azimuth east, along the shore of the Bay of Tranquility to hitchhike into Dirtweed. Trace the angle of deviation west as the crow flies to the baby schools; south by south west to the high school. In the heart of the town, where the action is, the river changes names again. Below the River of Joy, below the Purdy and well before the magnificent arrival into the Bay of Tranquility, the water turns black and mean and takes on the stink of creosote. Only the worst fish traverse downriver into the Bay or up-river to the lock: satiated monster carp gorge on spew from the pea-canning factory: undulating ribbons of pencil eels, urgent to arrive at the Purdy, poot out thousands of slippery spry; or, perhaps, the prehistoric sturgeon that somebody saw in '57. I hear it gets away. Slug-like lamprey hitch a ride, now up, now down, to commute in the current. Schools of pissed-off mudcat swim in lazy circles to forage or nestle motionless in sludge. Smell *the Fishn'Shit* in all her glory! She is on her own sudsy way around the bend; to flow under the "New Bridge", under the "Old Bridge" and filter naturally by the deep green waters of the Bay, where perch and pickerel, walleye and pike escape and evade in the freshness.

Clarence goes into Phil's Market to buy another popsicle. Like a raccoon, he fishes out two large pop bottles from the garbage drum, to make the deal. The clang of the bicycle rack splits his popsicle in two. The sound startles me.

"Want half?" he grins.

In the Holy Trinity of One Soul, Phil's Market is the Father, the Handy Dandy is the Son, and Bryce's at the far end, is the Divine Proceeding. The whole scene bursts open now in glorious technicolour. It is mine for the taking and I take great pleasure when I hear the melody of this glossy streetscape. In a moment, the sidewalk becomes a symphony composed by grinning boys and girls. They stop, rest, dart and for all the world, skate like water bugs across a Sea of Galilee. Like a hundred Jesuses populating a Currier and Ives print. The sun is up in the corner and the air is filled with the mechanical whine of cicadas. It is all sound and colour with me. "I love it so much, I love it!" I tell Clarence in the illiteracy of exuberance.

"We look like polliwogs to me" is how he sees it.

Well, he is right. We do look like polliwogs. The polliwogs are everywhere. I sit on warm cement and watch a girl draw a world class hopscotch board. Boys complain they need four legs to jump it.

"This is why you are apes," she says as a matter of fact.

Up and down, I see boys pretend to be superman. Capes knot around their necks. They jump from top steps and break their arms. Some have plastic jungle-fighter machine guns, locked and loaded. The crack of caps fills our ears. To a man, we groan, go down in a heap and die a thousand deaths. Boys dig marble holes with the heels of their black and white running shoes. They mould and smooth the rim; dig it deeper with their fingernails and play for *purees* and *cat's eyes*. A good ball bearing from the derricks is fair trade. It is worth a *conker* and three *milkies*, depending on the kid. Everyone makes deals.

I stop to flick my baseball cards against a brick wall. One twists to rest upright on its edge. Not a single girl, not a single boy can knock it down. I leave with a pile and scramble the cards high over my head. They flutter and soar. Clarence the Lion and I watch while urchins scramble to collect them. Ball hockey is in full rough and tumble glory. I curse and move the net whenever a car comes. Everyone collects *Brook Bond Tea* cards and pastes them into booklets of outer space, wild animals, earth shaking events or birds of North America. An enterprising boy from *Tanglefoot Acres* stands in the pathway between the houses that lead to the *Evergreens*. He sells Meadowlark Cigars for a quarter each to three mop-tops. It is Pinky, Joel-the-Hole and Bleeder. We pretend to be spastic when none of us thinks to bring a match. (*Buh dee chee chee.*) Greaseballs ride south on their motorcycles. Townie Teens with long hair, forever stuck in the time lock of their own destiny, play *Link Wray's Jack the Ripper* on transistor radios. The kids think they are stupid. A cluster of schoolmates draw out a big circle to play *Conquer the World*. I watch them print their countries in the earth with a broken branch stripped from a bloody bush across the road. The game is good. Darkness falls, the street lights come on and soon, the children disperse in dribs and drabs for home. Older boys stand and smoke in the shadows. Finally, it is just Clarence and I and we are back up by the bicycle stand at Phil's. We sit on the steps and watch hundreds of June bugs, whir by and bash into anything that glows. The nighthawks come then, to rip through the blackness: their cry distinctive, to make a swift appearance through buttery cones of lamplight. Heat lightning beholds the full majesty of indigo clouds and always, when the night grows humid, the stink of creosote seeps into our nostrils. It is good to be back on Eldorado.

There are three solar atmospheres around the stores on our small stretch of paradise. Phil's atmosphere is nice. It is clean and run by a ma and pa, whose three daughters all have Little Orphan Annie cartoon-hair, tight and always in place. I predict each of them will be a doctor or a surgeon somewhere, well beyond *Oncewuz*. They are that smart. Mrs. Phil is well-liked by the entire block and runs the checkout. She is tall and blocks the view of the candy counter behind her. It cascades up, almost to the ceiling. She makes a better door than a window. All you do is hand her a hastily scrawled note and some money: "*Dear Mrs. Phil. Please give Bleeder two packs of Du Maurier Kings and a sack of honeymoons.*" We feel the acceptance, the understanding and the warmth in that store. Everything is nice and orderly and they do not look at you twice if you come in five times a day with empty pop bottles. If there is a river watering the expanse of Eden, this is the variety store guarded by the fiery swords of cherubim. Now serving Little Pest number 23 and all that.

The *Handy Dandy* is different all together. Of the three, the Dandy is the only joint that sells firecrackers on Firecracker Day. It is run by whoever is on duty. It is always somebody we do not recognize. Depending on who it is, we do not need a note to buy smokes, either. The firecrackers are stacked in plain view on the counter, in their red cellophane. We can touch them, crinkle the wrappers and lust after them. The candy is behind glass and the glass is smeared with the whorls of a thousand eager fingerprints. Yum. The pop is in a giant cooler in the middle of the store. On summer days, in our search for currency, we learn to pull into the Dandy and mill about.

"Hey Pinky, I think I'll have a pop, want one?" someone might say.

This takes the pressure off to approach the cooler. I lift the hatch and run my hand along the tin-coated bottom. With cold water up to my elbows, I sweep for dimes and quarters. When anyone finds a dime: *finders' keepers, losers' weepers.* Still, there is something about the Handy Dandy that practically urges me to steal. It is part of the trap-line in *Oncewuz.*

"Hey Arse-face. How much did you pay for that?"

"Nothing. It's on sale. Five finger discount, Bub!" is the local joke.

There is as much going on outside as inside at the Dandy. It is seated at a crossroads, unlike Phil's which is on the way out of town. In the excitement of leaving the block, it is a comfort to rush into Phil's, say hi-and-bye and head off into oblivion. At the crossroads, however, there is ample entertainment. We just come to watch sometimes. There are no signs to tell you not to loiter. All kinds of characters flow in from the north and the south, the east and the west. In the days before apps, when boys walk the earth, hanging around is a skill.

Clarence and I notice today that the Greaseballs are out in full force. All of them sit on their rides, each bike tilts at a rakish angle. For all the world, they look funny in their armour: part god-like and part one hundred percent pure arse. We watch them screw off the gas caps, put their digit in the tank, whip out their Zippos with their good hands and immolate their thumbs. There is a low murmur across the tension and then fireballs of laughter, when a Greaseball breaks down and slaps out the flame on his dirty jeans. These manly arts make us giddy. When we grow bored, we approach the Greaseballs and tease them. They tolerate us for a while. One feints getting off his bike and they laugh when we scatter like chickens. Clarence and I can't help ourselves and join in. Suddenly, we are amidst a pack of boys who dash breakneck for sanctuary up towards Phil's. Like deer, some of us bound off down laneways or through backyards we know have no fence. Most of the time, the Greaseballs do not or cannot not keep up, but today they get Squeak. Like pirates they threaten to cut off his nuts. We watch from behind trees and hold onto our sides to keep our lungs in. Clarence and I yell and try to flush them; but in the end, we can do nothing to save Squeak. Unceremoniously, they pick him up like a sack of potatoes. They carry him past the bike stand and dump his sorry arse upside down into the fifty-gallon drum outside Phil's. He fits clean in. When Mrs. Phil opens the "Bubble Up, Seven Up" door to her store, the demons flit off, back down the street to the Handy Dandy. Like amplified farts, the motorcycles all start up in unison and the flatulent Greaseballs head off downtown to the Filbert, or somewhere else to find something to do.

Clarence and I go to fetch Squeak and help him out of the garbage drum. We brush him off as best as we can and give him the gears for getting caught. He is such a *whussy*. We know he will get the flyswatter on his legs for the fudgsicle stains on his tee-shirt. Chocolate is a bitch to get out.

Oncewuz is no different from most places. We only walk where we need to. We repeat it so many times that well-worn ruts of cattle trails appear in the soil. They run north to the River of Joy, south to the Bay of Tranquility, east up to the toboggan hill or in a westerly direction to the Baby Park.

Clarence and I hope to catch up to Fizzy, Marcel and Bumbo. We decide instead, after the dust settles and the Greaseballs are well out of harm's way, to amble up to the third congregation point—the Divine Proceeding known as Bryce's Variety. The Divine Proceeding is at the outskirts of Eldorado. To pass this spot is to commit to a walk downtown to The Bowels, or farther up, to the high school. At a right angle, a street makes an incline towards the Baby School. It takes seven minutes as the crow flies, to walk past the stately oaks and the maples and arrive on time in the school yard. All of us collect leaf specimens for our project. Bryce's is a weigh station. It is a space to congregate with enough time to make it before the bell; or it is an oasis of relief once the school day is over. A waterhole to pause and spoil our suppers. Clarence and I both order two scoops of cherry ice cream on a cone. "When things go bad," Clarence the Sweet-eyed Lion says, "my mom meets me right here. She knows enough not to come down to the schoolyard. I cry and all that shit and Mom buys me a cone and we walk home together. That is the one thing that keeps me in school."

"Clarence, I'm sorry," I say.

"*And the other, I don't care ...*" he sings.

We grow quiet for a time, concentrate and cock our heads to lick our cones around the base for drips. We amble back, the way we came. We pass the Handy Dandy and all is quiet on the western front.

We pull up at the little hedge that distinguishes Bumbo's house from the other houses on the block. There is a small porch at the front where he and his father like to sit and watch the street go by. Bumbo tells us how ballistic his dad gets when somebody tosses a candy wrapper into his hedge. Like seagulls, we constantly pick pop bottles out of there. Minus the hedge, the house is exactly like the house next to it, on either side. The mitosis continues up and down the block on both sides. Bumbo's little cousin comes for a visit, goes down to the Dandy, comes back and actually walks into the front door of the wrong house. The Storks have the nice house. It is a big grey stone extravaganza. A cement wall runs across the front. We sit aimlessly on it, eat *creamsicles* and kick our heals against the mortar. The Storks never run us off. We like that and are careful to pick up our wrappers, race across the street on one leg and deposit them into the drum at Phil's. The BadRicks live a couple houses up, beside Squeak and Pinky's. Old, hardworking, childless. I don't think I ever see them outside during the day. Mr. BadRick may be sighted at dusk, in his backyard, pruning his roses. It is like catching a glimpse of Bigfoot at the edge of a primordial forest. We simply marvel at what a colossal prick he is. I think at one point he has my football, about six of our softballs and probably thirteen badminton birdies. His yard and Pinky's overlook the Baby Park, with its beat-to-shit afterthought of a backstop. If you pop a foul high and back and it plops into BadRick's yard, the game completely grinds to a halt. The entire park grows silent, until laughter-begat curses bring expectations of sacrifice. Whoever loses the ball has to man-up or suck-out. I hate how loud a fence rings when you hoist yourself over it. Of course, everyone is quiet until the thump and roll on BadRick's side.

For a split, intimate second, I pick myself up and stand erect inside the perimeter. The ball, all innocent and come hither, is under some poppies. Committed now, I creep towards it. At this point Pinky, Squeak, Beamish, Bumbo, Marcel and Fizzy burst into war hoops. They kick any fence in sight to make it ring. Cringing, I grab the ball, pivot and fairly leap from ten feet out against the steel mesh. Up, over, careful not to crush my nuts, I hit the ground in a sprint. Everyone disperses again like deer. Some are down at the shack, others loll at a distance by the swings. BadRicks are out that day so I let the boys have it with both barrels. I fairly blast them with braggadocio. "Smell me!" I say.

In the days before apps, when boys walk the earth, the phrase becomes legend.

The next day, we realign our cosmos and blow the heads clean off his bastard poppies. We do anything we want with firecrackers on Pinky's side of the fence. Paybacks are a God-given right.

The song of hammering brings Clarence and I back to the middle of Bumbo's driveway. It is an unpaved strip that splits to a Y with a tiny garage at each side of the yaw. Tomato plants grow with pride along the outer sides, rhubarb along the back. Bumbo shows us how to snap off a red stalk, strip away the billowy green head-leaf and dip the end into a little glass of sugar. Despite all warnings I stop dipping only when a sugar-chancre forms on the inside of my lip.

Bumbo has the type of dad that doesn't make him hold the rag. He actually demonstrates how a thing should go and then lets him try it. In *Oncewuz*, the houses are all afterthoughts. Story-and-a-half nothings, slapped up to accommodate the boom. Most of them have asbestos shingles on their sides. Hard ridged rectangles, the consistency of slate, that clack when you stack them and give you shivers when you slide one off. Bumbo holds one in place for his dad and his dad hammers it in. Soon the air is filled with the sound of hundreds of hammers. *Tap tap tap* and a satisfied bang. *Tap tap tap* and a satisfied bang. A call and response that has the back and forth effect of bird warble somewhere in treetops across the road. Clarence the Lion and I watch the construction for a while.

Marcel Marceau strides up, out of the blue. He always seems to materialize, erect, like an exclamation mark. It startles the hell out of me. Fizzy is still at the Baby Park, waiting for us to come up and get a game going.

Even though Marcel's vocal chords did not get born right, the rest of him is easy to talk to. We compare our favourite toys, when they are all ours and we don't have to share them with our class of school chumps. Time ceases to exist when sunlight streams through a window to illuminate beautiful things. Dust mites become snow falling on an orange train, with a thousand tiny cars between engine and caboose. Marcel kneels down, rests his cheek on the rug.

At every car he whispers: "You all set? You all set? You all set?" Until the caboose arrives and he sits up on his knees, satisfied to look along the line, take hold of the engine and chug out of the station. He is one of those lucky boys whose kooky noggin is filled with imaginary friends. They are not just single people: They are clans, really, one and a group at the same time, separate and distinct. "Who are your friends?" I ask him.

Without even blinking he names them for me. "The Boodies, The Wah-Wahs, The Wee Wees and The Be-bops."

He says it with such conviction, I am convinced I see them too.

Bumbo's dad breaks our train of thought. He says thanks and lets Bumbo go. Bumbo comes over to the edge of the driveway and stands around with Clarence, Marcel and I.

"Let's go up to the Baby Park," he says.

The sidewalk takes us to a path. The path cuts through the houses. It is bordered by brambles on both sides. The gravel is littered with a Hobo's Delight of Meadowlark cigars, half-smoked and crushed out. It is dark at first, cooler in the shade but the light opens like a trumpet bell to reveal a small warm field, shaped at random like a large slab of peanut brittle. There is a sandbox; a wooden shack, open with rafters to shield from the sun; beside that a cement house, locked and barred. It holds the tether balls, stilts, plaster of Paris, beads, bobbles and felt-the stuff of organized games.

We race like music then, across the open field, baseball diamond to the right, set of swings to the left, everything bordered by weeping willows. All the swings are taken. Fizzy has the last one and we see a boy, we do not know. Our antennae go up then and we gallop to a halt.

Perhaps the worst thing in the world is to wait for a swing. When you go to the swings, you need to swing. It is all that matters. When all four seats are occupied, a small eternity might pass before there is a vacancy. And the hell of it is, the kids on the swings understand the power they wield. The power possesses their face in little smirks and the way their eyes look at you, like googly eyes, on stalks, as the swing arcs up and returns. Back and forth, their stare is nothing short of a metronome that ticks off a rhythm of selfishness and the other Jimmy Crack Corn. Homicide pervades the atmosphere.

To be in possession of a swing and to know it, is to have bargaining power. Bumbo has a perfect peacock feather, traded by one of the boys at school—all for what? For a turn on the swing? Yes. A turn on a swing. Bumbo's mom frames it for posterity and we think he is lucky.

The strange boy talks to Fizzy. Fizzy stops the swing, dangles his legs and tips his toes off the sand. The effect is one of casual control. The boy says if Fizzy gives up the swing, he will give Fizzy a quarter. I practically see Fizzy do the calculations in his head. We all do the math. Twenty-five cents equal five large pop bottles or twelve and a half small bottes, give or take. A quarter is gold. Definitely no trade backs and I can tell Fizzy will take it. The strange boy holds the coin between his thumb and forefinger. Like a little kitten encouraged by treats, Fizzy gets off but keeps one hand on the chain of the swing. The strange boy steps back, arm out straight, but now Fizzy has to stretch. Fizzy grabs the quarter but the strange boy pinches it. We all want to wipe the grin off his alien face. Now he has his hand on the other chain of the swing. Fizzy pulls and pulls, there is a feral stink in the air and right when the boy puts his arse in the saddle, Fizzy tugs, yanks the quarter loose and we all run for the hills. The boy gives a half-hearted chase, looks over his shoulder and goes back to claim the swing before other kids hop on. We take off through the laneway over by the broken backstop, pass BadRick's yard and head straight over to Phil's.

Popsicles for all. Some of us make a note of the strange boy's technique for future reference. Certain skills in the schoolyard are a necessary evil. A deal is not always a deal.

We grow aimless then, and go home to get our gloves. Pinky brings his bat and we return to the Baby Park to play scrub. We pick up a couple of expendable boys along the way to fill out the bases, right, left and centre fields and still have enough for a pitcher. Each batter assumes catcher duties.

We do that for a while and then sit in the shade. Squeak knows how to make trumpet sounds from a blade of grass in his cupped hands. Clarence gets it before I do and Bumbo just never gets it. We all have a good laugh and give him the gears for it.

"*Buh dee chee chee*," he says.

We loll in the shade at the back of Stork's house. Their backyard is an orchard of lilac and honeysuckle, purple morning glory and pink bursts of flowering crab. Honey bees and fat Queens rule the space and the cicadas whine about it. A tall chain link fence separates our moment. We run our fingers carefully over metal barbs and inspect the steel honeycomb. The air is summer-warm and a breeze brings with it stories in small gusts.

Pinky remembers the day Squeak gets impaled not ten yards from where we rest.

"Squeaky pops a foul over Stork's fence, right into the middle of his yard. We all see it plop on the lawn. The guy who loses it has to go and get it. Period," he says, to punctuate the rule. Squeaky makes his leap, straddles the fence and holds himself up to protect his nuts. He throws his leg over, hops down, rolls for effect, grabs the ball and throws it back. We all get up, turn our backs and get ready to play. The fence sings as Squeaky pulls himself over. All of a sudden, he screams. *Jeezis Christ*! There he is, dangling by one hand. Do not ask me why they put sharp spear-heads on the top of chain-link fences in a ball park. "Do you remember running over to lift him off? Remember the point sticking clean through and all the blood? Dad is so pissed and takes him up to the hospital. He comes back looking like an oven mitt."

"Remember how we signed his cast?" I guffaw.

"*Dough-head.*"

"*Get better soon, Fake-er.*"

"*Better your hand, then your n**s!*"

"*To our ball-baby. Sniff-sniff, Boo Hoo.*"

It is all good for a laugh until Beamish tells my tale.

"We play scrub over by the shack because other kids occupy the baseball diamond. Bleeder hits a pitiful single and slides for first. Only he keeps sliding on the dew, down that trough over there and hangs his leg up on the bottom of the fence. Tears the meat right out of his calf and the barbs hold it up. He is so stupid he can't even cry. We run up to see if we can get his leg off and the meat is just peeled back. What does his brother do? Kicks the fence right in the arse, and Bleeder's leg falls free. His brother walks him home. What a baby and we don't see him again for another five years.

"You are an asshole," I laugh.

Marcel makes us cringe when he recounts the one where Joel-the-Hole plays Everest on the swings.

"Get this. He's on the swing. He scales up as high as he can go on the outside bar and pushes off twirling. He goes way out and it is all going well until he comes back and tries to get his feet back on the bar. Only his feet slip and he comes straight down on his nuts. That's why he talks like his sister now."

"You are an asshole," Joel-the-Hole laughs.

While we all talk falsetto, a garter snake glides over the grass in a perfect "S". The yellow stripe gives him away. We chase it for a while and box it in like pros. Clarence puts his foot on it and picks it up. Everyone gets a turn to inspect.

I look it dead in the eye, copy the flick of its red, monofilament tongue and like a skunk, it lets its odour go all over my left hand. I drop it and it takes off under Stork's fence.

"Nice going, Bleeder," somebody says.

Fizzy Jack tells me I stink and then everyone else laughs.

"Smell you!"

They bound away like white-tail deer and this provokes a game of tag for twenty minutes or so. After, we collapse in a heap, out of breath, in the clover. "Goose pile!" Beamish yells and together we crush Joel-the-Hole, like a bug.

Lewdly, somebody begins to sing:

Roll me o-ver. In the clo-ver
Roll me o-verrrrr. In the clo-verrrrr
Roll me over, in the clover
Lay me down and do it a-gain, Ugh Ugh Ugh!"

There it is. A stupid ditty stuck in my mind forever.

Clarence the Bright-Eyed Lion takes possession of the lost moment and embellishes the story of Fizzy and the Quarter. By re-telling the story, he sets it like a diamond in all of our minds. Fizzy has a fine ring to add to his treasure with the boys of *Oncewuz*.

"Let's play Shingle Tag!" Fizzy yells out of the blue.

In the days before apps when boys walk the earth, Bumbo gets a good one off. I see it the moment the little shingle leaves his fingertips. Viewed from the apex of the play shack, Bumbo's technique is perfect. He cocks his arm, bends back and with a beautiful snap of his wrist, releases the shingle at a perfect angle from his hip. The sheer velocity of the throw makes time stop. I track the projectile, from the ground up and see it correct its own course and like a guided missile, it makes sure. At the last second, I somehow manage to turn my head. What happens next is the stuff of lore: *The day Bumbo nails Jimmy playing shingle tag in the park.*

The way they tell it, I supposedly clap my hand over my right eye, swear and immediately go down on my back on top of the little shack in the Baby Park. The shack stands about 15 feet off the ground. It has rafters you can climb along. The roof is made of plywood sheeting and the boys and I modify it by turning a small break into a ragged hole that we can pull our whole body through to emerge on the angle of the slope. Moaning, flat on my back and helpless like a *whussy*, I slide down towards the edge. If Pinky doesn't grab me by the collar, I will fall clean off. A couple of the other boys help me down. I lay on the grass, cursing. The ripe indignity of blood trickles down my arm and in the process, destroys my favourite t-shirt. The boys are scared to see what lies underneath my hand. I refuse to move it away so they can inspect the damage. To break the tension and relieve his guilt, Bumbo tells me I am a fake and to smarten the hell up. Pinky pries my hand away. They all see the nick pulse with blood underneath my eyebrow. "Jimmy, you Arse. Your eye's alright but your face sure looks shitty!" This remark makes them all laugh, me too, and with effort, they help me to my sorry feet. I peel off my t-shirt and keep it over my eye. Two of the boys stay to smoke and Pinky takes me over to his place to clean up. We pass the huge metal swing set where Joel-the-Hole got it in the nuts last summer.

Pinky gets me in the back door. Thankfully his parents are on the veranda. Oblivious to our coming and going, they chat away. It is best they do not know what happens. Pinky's dad builds us a little room, by the furnace, with a card table to play board games on. The perfect congregation point, our Club I guess you can say, and little do we know that Mr. Pinky has a motive. *Green Ghost, Stratego, Dog Fight, Wide World, Conflict, Go to the Head of the Glass, The Game of Life* are all stacked squarely on a jerry-built utility shelf. By this time half of us smoke Meadowlark cigars that Brownie sells to us, one at a time for a profit. Still, we manage to get a game in Saturday nights, and twice on Sundays, if we get our homework done.

The playroom leads to the bathroom and it is here that I, Jimmy the Bleeder, fix myself up with cold water and Kleenex. I pray to *Jeezis* that the cut will not need stitches. It does not. Pinky puts my t-shirt in a grocery bag and stashes it away in the garbage can, outside. He loans me a fresh t- shirt and tells me not to get cooties on it. By now, the street lamps come on. June bugs are out again, in full force. If you are lucky, you might see another nighthawk pierce the air and swoop through the humidity. Careful to guard my face, I say a quick hello-goodbye to Pinky's parents and make my way down The Street of Gold to home. Along the driveway, past the asbestos shingles, I enter by the back door, kick off my runners and make a quick right up the stairs to my room. My father is in the kitchen.

"Hi Jimmy! Did you behave yourself today, son?"

How strange. I feel unreal, as if my father somehow, already has the word on Shingle Tag. In my mind I translate his hello as: "... *and if you are not careful, one of you boys will put an eye out.*" The Old Boy always seems to be on top of it. Everyone is in *Oncewuz*. Neighbourhood watch and all that malarkey. One phone call is all it takes. Reach out and squeal on somebody.

"Yes, Dad" is all I say. What else can I say?

My brother is upstairs in his room and listens to LP records. He is back from somewhere. With an uncanny ability that accelerates his years, he asks me what the fuck happened to my eye? I spill the beans. My brother laughs and calls me an Arse for playing shingle tag in the first place. There it is. I get it from both barrels. Everybody is a parent. Later, I phone Jim's Pizza to order a medium bacon and peperoni with change from pop bottles, supplemented with allowance money. It is my idea. I am magnanimous. It takes a full week before my brother realizes his t-shirt is missing.

There is still some time left in the day. Like apes, we leave the Baby Park and troop out to the street. We head north passed Phil's down a gravel path that separates neighbourhoods. We don't really know anyone down in *Tanglefoot Acres*. We don't really need to.

There is a part of us that is jealous because the houses are nicer, the driveways are separate and everything looks clean and sharp. The road curves and takes us to a row of houses fronting the rind of a field. There is a narrow space between two homes, a muddy path that opens up to grassland, bull reeds, vernal ponds and polliwogs. We traverse a board walk, swat mosquitos and blue tail flies and spill out to a stand of trees we dub *The EverGreens*. We migrate to the "counting bush" and some of us share a Meadowlark. Mister Marceau volunteers to be 'it' so we turn our backs and send him into the trees to hide. There is a time when girls blip onto our radar. When our brothers start dating, we grow sheepish to play Werewolf. At a certain point, we know our Baby Game days are numbered. There just might be other things to do on a Friday night but for now, our experience is sweetly wrapped in innocence. Still, life begins to cull the herd. The siren call is gentle. Boys decide to do something else, slowly at first and then, a certain disdain catches hold of us so quickly, not one of us looks back. Fewer boys show up to play and after a while nobody does.

Ironically, the diaspora begins over an organized game. Squeak makes the first concession and gets the idea to join a baseball league. All the major businesses field a team: the Bakery, the Creosote Plant, the Auto Wreckers, the Cops, the Root Beer Joint. We call the Bakery Boys the Chelsea Buns out of contempt. Squeaky comes back like he joins the Marines or something. He tells us how to sign up so we all do. It is a mistake. Impersonally, our group is divided. Fizzy, Beamish and I get on with the Root Beer Joint and the rest of us get on with the Cops. Of course, the Cops have connections everywhere. They stack their team with every six-foot monkey in town. A roster circulates. Some of us play on Wednesday night and some of us play on Friday night. We worry that none of us are around anymore for scrub or shingle tag. The Cops clean up. They win the little trophy. This is largely because of the Arse we elect as Mister FunFair along with the help of his big brother. Fizzy, Beamish and I get sugar-chancres from all the free game-time root beer. Most of us hate it. The rest grow up.

Joel-the-Hole and Pinky get on with the air cadets of *Oncewuz*. For some unknown reason the Old Boy won't give me permission.

Fizzy, Bumbo, Clarence, Marcel and I are left to hold the bag. I grouse to my brother and he tells me to get over it. Later I overhear the Old Boy tell the Old Girl how a century ago a scout leader diddled two townie boys. It is the first time we hear the word: *diddle.* We make note of the language and bring it into our lexicon. In the days before apps when boys walk the earth, few of us fathom a scout Ape wanting to touch our *doinks.* Pinky and Joel-the-Hole assure us that their *doinks* are fine and we lose both of them for an entire summer.

Tonight, we have each other. We are smarter than we look. We know Werewolf is a rite of passage—a natural progression to wilder, darker time and space, where everything will change: friends, attitude, meaning, lifestyle and look. We love where we are together. There really is no need for a future. A moment is more urgent.

"I have to go," Joel-the-Hole announces.

"Not again!" Fizzy says.

"Nature hath called," he grins.

There is something in the perfume of cedar trees that infests Joel-the-Hole and no matter what, he has to take a dump. We name the Toilet Tree exclusively for him, far to the left of the Counting Bush. Before we even think to enter the *EverGreens* to flush Marcel, we all search our pockets for Kleenex. Bumbo usually drools so we count on him to have some; but for the rest of us, it is a longshot. We wait and wait for Joel-the-Hole to sheepishly emerge. In time, we stop teasing him and just accept him as fact. We all have our quirks that way.

The art of Werewolf is to fan out, find Marcel and not get caught. Small trails run in a mishmash through the cedars with myriad places to hide. At dusk, the camouflage is natural. The chickens flock to the perimeter but a few brave souls walk straight in on point. I am right beside Marcel Marceau when he grabs my leg. Caught like a rat. "Werewolf! Werewolf!" I howl.

So now there are two monsters. Marcel and I fan out to search and destroy. It is acceptable at this point for anyone to find a favourite hiding hole and observe others get caught and eaten. The courtesy is to not remain hidden for two days. It is also a skill to flush, keep moving and hide somewhere new. This goes on until the last Ape is caught. The last Ape tends to milk it and see if he might evade seven or eight werewolves to eternity. When boredom sets in, when the game is obviously won, the victorious survivor now places himself at risk. It is an expectation to return to the Counting Bush, fire up a Meadowlark, search around for stones and heave them into the trees. Squeak sends a rock in. It is an unbelievably lucky shot and nails Pinky on the shoulder. He screams, comes out and charges his brother like a bull in a ring. There is a ruthless intimacy to his anger. We peel them apart. Repeat to infinity.

By now, the peepers are out in full chorus. In the humidity, they sound like rain. Time is spirit-form in *Oncewuz* and defined by how we feel. The game is over. We are tired. It is time to head home, period. Nobody needs a watch. The streetlights are on and have been on a little too long. The air is damp. Sweat brings its chill. We march through plumes of smoke, single file, over duckboard, out the muddy path and onto the streets of *Tanglefoot Acres*. The bats are out now and we stop our headlocks and piggybacks to watch them have their demonic way with unseen mosquitoes. I love how they flutter and strafe the street. Up and down, to the side, down low, over our heads. I get a good look at one or two when they dance through the lamp light. "They look like you, Fizzy," some expendable boy says.

None of us laugh and nobody says: *"Buh dee chee chee."* Expendable Boys often overstay their welcome after a game. Sure, we need them to flesh out the fun, like we need them to play a good game of scrub in the Baby Park; but all said and done, they revert to strangers after the laughter goes. It is a relief when they make their own way home.

"Who invited them?" I ask Squeak

"Not sure," he says. "Maybe Pinky, hard to know."

By now it does not matter. They drift off in shadows as we round the bend to head up the laneway to Phil's and the honey-glow of Eldorado. We disperse along cattle trails to war-time homes and murmur vague plans to meet tomorrow.

Morning arrives, all cartoons end and there is a knock at my door.

"When are you going up to Dug Hill?" Fizzy asks in his jerky way on the front porch.

"Not sure," I hear myself say. "Do you feel like going downtown into The Bowels?"

Fizzy likes the idea for lack of any other idea. The screen door slams and we are out on the sidewalk. What ho! Like a lobster in a trap, Fizzy plucks a two-cent bottle from the hedge.

I cannot get the cartoons out of my head and it is at this exact point that Bumbo appears in the milk wagon. Old Gray takes his dump. I watch with fascination as the road apples plop down one by one, to mash upon the road. It is not something you see everyday.

We turn right at the crossroads down at the Handy Dandy. The air fills with the transistor crackle of song. I hear surf pound and watch seagulls beak-stab one another in the head over French fries. The Greaseballs are back to immolate their thumbs. Two of them turn to look at us.

"Don't provoke them, Jimmy," Fizzy says.

I don't and they turn away uninterested.

Old Gray takes us west along Dicky Street. Dicky Street is the main road, over the New Bridge. It is one of two gateways into The Bowels. There is always a line up at the Old Bridge to let the yachts and sailboats through. They make their wobbly way north along the Fishn'Shit, past the Creosote Plant, under the high arch of the New Bridge and up to the lock at the Purdy. It is Purdy easy to get through and together they tack up to the River of Joy. The River of Joy sails them north, against the current, far up to Muskie Country where cottages become camps and every boy gets a .303 for his tenth birthday. That is what I hear, anyway.

The clink of milk bottles brings me to. Fizzy has a handful of paperclips, the large ones, and twists them in two. He increases his yield an hundredfold. I hold out both hands in a cup and collect a whack of what now look like tiny trombone slides. I carefully shift them to one hand and stuff them into the pouch of my kangaroo sweatshirt, complete with hood for anonymity. Bumbo pulls out three office rubber bands, the sturdy and thick kind. He hands one each to Fizzy and me. I see we are about to play Twelve O'clock High.

Twelve O'clock High may also be played on foot, so long as I walk fast and constantly look over my shoulder. The technique is gloriously simple: Stretch the rubber band across thumb and forefinger. Hook the trombone slide carefully over both strands of rubber band and pull back for distance. Do not point it at someone's eye. This is for keeps and more dangerous than shingle tag. (The hood of my kangaroo sweatshirt is already up.) Aim particularly, at the metal base of a screen door and fire for effect. The trombone slide makes a nice *thunk*. It is prudent to do this from a distance; otherwise, there is a chance a dent will appear. The art is to keep it as a game as opposed to a felony. Only an arse wants to cause damage and this is why we play Twelve O'clock High nowhere near the Street of Gold.

"Messerschmitt at eleven!" Fizzy yells. *Thunk.*

"Fokkewulf at two!"

"I got it Jimmy." *Thunk.*

And so on.

We pass the cop shop, the fried chicken place, the bowling alley and the root beer joint.

"Lights on for service!" Bumbo yells.

In the days before apps when boys walk the earth, there is a restaurant where we pull in on an angle, or back in on an angle. Unless we turn our lights on, a waitress will not come out and serve us. The burgers are good here, the fries even better, hold the onion rings and like I say, the root beer is guaranteed to give you a sugar chancre if you down two, back to back.

"What the hell is going on here. Are they asleep?"

"Turn the lights on, Jimmy, you arse."

"Whups."

Old Gray takes us over the top of the New Bridge and Bumbo brings him to a halt.

The breeze is beautiful up here. I look downriver, where the Fishn'Shit runs clean. A sailboat comes through where the Old Bridge cantilevers at right angles to the road.

Behind that, a big-water yacht peaks single file, around the mast. I feel its frustration. It is anxious to get out and ahead and away from the confines of *Oncewuz.* Beyond that I see the Bay of Tranquility. The sunny dapple of sparkling water obscures outboard fishermen and sun-bathing pleasure craft. I spy old apple orchards on the far bank and rich houses along a Bay which curves out of sight, under white clouds.

I stand on the milk wagon and turn my gaze upriver. It is here the Fishn'Shit is at its worst. It laps the long north bank of the Creo-sote Plant. The breeze is warm and strong and goosebumps form on my arms. Wind current from the bend up by the Purdy, brings the stink of chemicals right inside my nostrils. Fizzy sneezes and Bumbo wipes his drool on his sleeve. To my right, women and their men shore-fish from lawn chairs. A kid snags his line on an overhanging tree and it looks like he is going to pull the tree into the water.

I rub the back of my neck and look skyward. The motion takes my gaze over the black train bridge, up into a white orb of sun. I squint. I see two hawks but the light changes the birds of prey into two boys with feathers. Fizzy sees it too. One boy is higher than the other. They escape the gravity and see *Oncewuz* in her full Techni-color glory: her warts and her beauty. It is as if she is a siren, seduc-tive, scaly, topless. It is as if she is Auntie Peach-Pit, safe, bossy and laughing. All of the children along the bank look up now. We cannot help it. Before our eyes, the top-boy faulters. His left-wing breaks in a burst of feather specks and he plummets like a meteorite. There is a violent explosion of white froth on the surface of the river. The other boy hovers alone in the sky. The wind returns and he banks over the Dug Hill to sail like a tiny condor, north by north west to a fate unknown. Fizzy, that bastard actually throws his arm around my shoulder and says something nice about my brother.

"I know four or five guys like that," he whispers.

"*... and the other I don't care,*" Bumbo says for me.

Old Gray stamps and whinnies. All of us swish the blue tail flies away from his head with our hickory brooms. Tongue-clicks goad the horse on. The clip-clops take us over the crest, down the other side of the New Bridge to the west bank of The Bowels of *Oncewuz*. We alight and run to water's edge. Across the span of the Fishn'Shit we see Marcel. He stands on a rick of creosote ties and waves to us from the far side of the river.

We talk to the man with a white helmet. Mister Marceau recom-mends us and we hire on for the summer. Three forty-four an hour. Bring your lunch and lots of water.

We have no idea where we are. Black-stained men in coveralls shuffle from point A to point B. They are in no hurry to get anywhere. On the other hand, we are in a complete hurry to start work; to wonder what the job will be and to do our best. What to men appears as a colossal mess of greasy railroad ties on skids, appears to boys as a competition for territorial rights. Who can pull out twenty, one at a time and run them to the end of the skids? Who can 'rick' them into bales, band them, crimp them, howl at the moon and move on to the next rick? Today, it is Clarence the Hard-Working Lion and Bleeder versus Marcel and Bumbo. Fizzy gets the easy job in the white tie mill. He throws clean railroad ties off rollers onto a ribbed tram. For ten cents more an hour, he uses chalk to mark each tie and record the tally on a clipboard. When we find this out, we are ruthless.

"Fizzy, how do you get this job? You cannot count that high, boy."

"At least our muscles grow manly, while you turn into the shrimp."

And so on.

By the third day, we have second thoughts. Creosote no longer wafts in the air over The Street of Gold on humid evenings, it sweats out of our pores. We stink, in other words. Our muscles ache and complain in the morning. Still we show up. It is unthinkable to quit.

Clarence and I get a bag of five hundred "S-irons" each. We march to the north yard to pound them into the ends of railroad ties to keep them from splitting. We are sent there by a man in an off-white helmet whom everyone jokes about behind his back. We see why. We have not met an incompetent adult before. He is a novelty. On the way to the north yard, we pass clusters of scruffy men who stand in the shade, hide out, avoid work and drink Mickeys well into Friday afternoon. These same men regularly attend union meetings. They fight for their rights and the coffee is pretty good over there. I know, because Fizzy and I have to clean toilets and mop down the kitchenette.

Clarence and I bang S-irons into the ends of railroad ties, all afternoon, until the man with the real white helmet stops by to check on us.

"Why are you two assholes pounding irons into soft ties?" he barks.

The tone stings us.

"Don't you know you pound them into hard ties?"

"We do what we are told, Boss," Clarence says.

"Well, you have been told wrong. Grab your shit and follow me!"

I notice that the cluster of men that are in the north yard with us disperse to their stations. There is not a Mickey in sight.

Clarence and I find ourselves in the back of a half-sided railroad car. Fizzy is demoted and is in a second car with Bumbo. We sit on the top edge as far as we can from the front. A crane lowers a gaggle of stinking creosote ties straight out from the ovens. They cook off in the heat. The load clangs off the front end and the entire box car shudders. I feel it in my fillings. I take off the fastener on the cable and race to the back end. In principle the man in the crane lifts the load slowly, and the entire mess disperses along the floor of the railroad car. Our job is to smooth them all out for the next layer. By the third load, three of us learn to climb completely out of the car and hide between the couplings for protection. Bumbo learns this by the fourth load after the hook on a swinging cable nearly removes his head.

At the end of the day, we race home, turn left at the Handy Dandy onto the Street of Gold and leave our bicycles in the driveway. We strip to our undies in back yards and put the hose on our clothes. The rest of the night we scrub dirty creosote blotches off our forearms and out from under our fingernails. It is a complete waste of time. The filth of creosote is replaced by the pungent stink of varsol. Charmed, I'm sure.

By the end of our stay, we learn to shuffle. We are in no hurry to get anywhere fast. We are short-timers and the men forgive us. There are no hello's and goodbyes. We arrive and we disappear. Just like that. In the trick of light, we are not yet men but no longer really boys. We are somewhere in between, flush with money. Not a single one of us scrounge for pop bottles again.

By now, Old Gray disappears. The five of us watch smoke rise by the Old Bridge and we walk east along the main drag to investigate.

In a parking lot, by the arena, we pass a midway. The carnies are in town.

Each year, like clockwork, they bring with them a light rain. Like it or not, the two things we count on in *Oncewuz* is: it always rains on carnie weekend and it always rains on Firecracker Day. There is no use fighting it. The light rain makes the blinking red and green lights glisten. The drone from the diesel engines that propel the rides is rendered mute. The sound is replaced by a smear of laughter while bells ring and harmonize with the hum of kazoos. Children are everywhere. They eat taffy apples and candy floss. Large stuffed panda's hitch a ride on the back of strollers. The Greaseballs run the place and there is a vague malevolence to their presence in this happy sea of innocence. I want to try the rides. We start with the *Tilt-a-whirl* and jump off the *Octopus* after Fizzy and I sit in some puke on a seat. The boys give us the gears. None of them stand next to us until the joke wears off. Marcel Marceau gives away his extra tickets to a random kid and we leave in a pack to check out the smoke by the Old Bridge.

Behold the conflagration! The Bowels are on fire, yet somehow, we breathe through the smoke. We are unaffected by the heat and protected from the flames. The inferno is cold, indifferent and practically biblical in proportion. Like Daniel, we move through a lion's den, untouched. The record store by the wharf, goes up first and with it, a trove of 45 rpm records. The post office crumbles into ember. All that is left is a phallic clock tower which transforms into a municipal office. Flames hopscotch over the cinema and take out the Filbert, even before we get a chance to sneak into the *Men's Entrance* for a cocktail. We are jealous of the *Gentlemen and Escorts* door, which is a laugh, noting the Filbert begat the Sherwood Forest which begat a strip joint. None of us has a girl friend anyway. By the time we arrive, the German Bakery is decimated and with it, the finest Chelsea buns that ever pop out of an oven. All the specialty stores go up, the Egg Grading Station and the Butcher Shop. The bus depot beside the malt shop still stands and it is in our mind now to take the Shopper's Bus and get the hell out of town.

The fellow that sells day tickets to *Neverwuz* scares us. Beastly, he is a minotaur: half man, half Arse: the last man on earth anyone admits knowing. His unshaven jaw and white marine hair-do, bristles like hair on the butt of a pig. He is known to fart at will and insists on wearing a stained t-shirt over his pot belly. He is gruff as a border guard. One of those can't-just-sell-you-a-ticket-what-is-the-purpose-of-your-visit type of certified Apes. For a second, I don't think I will be permitted to leave *Oncewuz*. The boys pony up and under duress, I get five-day tickets to *Neverwuz*.

"Make sure you hooligans get the last bus out; otherwise bring a dime to call your mommies," he sneers.

"Buh dee chee chee," Fizzy replies.

Outside, we share a Meadowlark to get the smell of fart out of our nostrils. The Shopper's Bus pulls up beside the police station. We are thrilled by its leviathan presence. The engine rumbles, the air stinks of diesel, the door sucks open and single file we scale the steps to find seats at the back. The bus purrs for a while and then swings out in slow motion. We are compelled to leave. It is inevitable.

Before we depart, somewhere between the main street and the bus depot, I manage to slip into the hobby store before it too, burns down. I buy the last two tins of pellets, five hundred shots to a can. One for Fizzy and one for me. Out of all of us, Fizzy is the one who has a dog, whose parents know how to fly-fish, whose brother knows how to skin a squirrel, stretch the hide on a board and salt it.

We appear at Fizzy's grandfather's tobacco farm with a day to roam and orders to return at supper time. The best way to store lead pellets is to put twenty of them in your mouth. I crack the pellet gun, take out a pellet, slide it into the hole for a seamless fit, snap the barrel back and I am set. We begin with the vegetable kingdom. It is easy to prune the sucker leaves off a tobacco plant. A clean shot through the stem drops the leaf: one pellet if I sharp-shoot, three or four if I am sloppy. We de-evolve and notice the insect kingdom. Brown grasshoppers are huge. Perpendicular to rows, their exoskeleton stands out like a battleship. I aim a quarter inch in front of the broadside and send twenty of them into oblivion. I re-load. Insulator glass on telephone wires is impossible to break, so we switch to a string of swallows. They go down like tin ducks at the midway. A train goes by and we shoot it. Finally, by the irrigation pond, we stalk leopard frogs and nail our fill. Minnows swarm them in the water and nibble the babies to pieces. By dusk, I take aim at a sparrow in a birch tree. Last pellet, last shot and I take her beak off. The sparrow drops to my feet in a swirl of pain and feathers. I do my frantic best to put it out of its misery with my gun butt. I miss and the little bird hurls itself over a rise into the bushes to die somewhere quietly with my childhood.

We arrive in *Neverwuz*. All the buses growl in the terminal. We cut through a busy soda fountain where sun light streams the length of the counter and we make our way over to the main drag. On a corner we circle the wagons to take stock. The block looks nothing like our Eldorado. There is a mob of stores with everything to sell. They yell at us to come hither and buy. A shady fellow in a brown monk's frock hands me a pamphlet. He invites me to join his weirdo church and feel better. I feel good enough already so I throw it out. Fizzy keeps his as a souvenir from *Neverwuz*. A tramp asks Bumbo for any spare change. Bumbo is wise to decline because between the five of us, I think we have eighteen dollars. On my side of a steam-y glass window, food I have not seen before makes me hungry; but we stick to pop and chips for now. Clarence the Tough-Eyed Lion fires up a Meadowlark. He fits in here. Everyone is city-strange but Clarence smiles and looks content. Marcel consults a piece of paper with an address on it. We are too stupid to know where north is so I ask. A guy says it is a long walk and points to the subway. I won't admit it, but I am scared of the subway, so we cross over to walk on the sunny side of the street. We walk past Greaseballs, freaks and tough looking street kids. They congregate around a storefront community centre and despite the sun, look chilly and flu-ridden. Everyone smokes so we do too. See the townie tourists live like there is no tomorrow in *Neverwuz*. We pass our seventh set of subway stairs and still we head north like men of iron; to stop, now and then to gawk at drug paraphernalia and manikins in leather.

"Surf's up on the sea of sin!" Fizzy says and we all laugh.

Finally, we get to the Record Shop and I am under strict orders to ask for a bootleg copy of Link Wray and His Wraymen.

"You know, the stuff in the back!" Marcel says in a parody of the Three Stooges.

We all feel like Stooges but who cares? The long-haired cat reaches down under the counter and pulls up a non-descript white album cover. With pride, he slips out the contraband rim of a green vinyl record. It is all top secret. I make the deal and feel more like a hero than a crook.

Nobody has a watch so we ask the time. Fizzy checks his ticket and says we should head back to the bus terminal.

"Who's for the subway?" I say.

There are no takers and I am glad.

"Got the 'fraidy-cat in ya, eh?" I taunt.

"Buh dee chee chee," they respond, correctly and on cue.

We cross the road to catch up to the sunny side and walk south in a gaggle. There is a shop with glass pipes and cannabis belt buckles.

"Wait up, fellas," Clarence the Red-Eyed Lion says.

We loiter in front of the shop for a while. I see fruits I have no idea what to call so Fizzy buys an apple. Finally, Clarence emerges.

"Check these out," he says.

He displays a handful of cigarette rolling papers. Some have leopard skins, some are hundred-dollar bill replicas and some look like they are already tripping.

"I collect them," Clarence says.

"Whatever," we say.

The porn shop and a crosswalk are our bread crumbs and we know the bus station is a block over. There is enough time to grab a burger and a shake at the diner.

Exhaustion is indifferent to time as we feel the bus make its lazy roundabout into the parking lot, beside the police station in *Once-wuz*. (I point out *"The Place of Four Fingers"* on the way back.) The door swishes open. On cramped legs we descend. The clouds have that dark blue silhouette look. Night must come. The smell of smoke replaces the stink of creosote and I see the town still burns.

The milk wagon is gone. We are not on bikes. I am not sure what we are on. *Oncewuz* is an ember that glows like breath when the wind kisses it. I want to kiss it. By now the bid is lost. The big mall is fully built and bustles to the east of us, in Dirtweed. Box stores suck my town dry like a Fishn'Shit leech. Even the kids see it. Plain and simple: *Oncewuz* got her arse kicked: A ghost town gone angel.

Three of the five us are thirsty. We pick our way through what is left of the Filbert and enter the Sherwood Forest.

"You urchins go in through *the Babies and Escorts* door," I deadpan to Clarence and Bumbo.

The night is mute. Expectantly, we open the door to an explosion of noise, beer-scent, lit cigarettes and social gaggle. There are girls present. To a soul, they all look up when we enter, then turn away. I am disappointed. The return to *Oncewuz* from the city changes the game. I pass through a portal into a time warp. One or two Grease-balls stand: perennials at the bar. They look sullen and ready to shit-kick. We avoid their gaze. Everyone else grows their hair long and to an Ape, will keep it this way for decades. They will never get out and to be honest, I tell Fizzy that I envy that. Four or five No-minds from the Base, clean-cut and pimply, sit near the biffies. We all co-exist in this atmosphere. It is beautiful, really. The esprit des corps of drink-ing. We are not friends, yet we are not enemies. We are *compadres* in the old Sierra Madres. We share space for an evening and we mean nothing to one another tomorrow, but it sure feels great tonight.

Mister Marceau finds us a table and I go up to get rum and coke for the Boys and a shot, no mix for Fizzy. Some nights we have to look out for our merry man. Especially at The Sherwood Forest.

A roadie sets up the stage and a piano chord announces a town-ie Battle of the Bands. (What ho! "Next week, Max Webster!") It is noisy until a good-looking girl mounts the stage to ask us to "give a big welcome to Smile." We do. Smile takes the stage. The drummer hops into his kit, the lead guitarist straps in and tweaks his amp, the bass player *buh, boop boo's* a triplet. Kablam! They are off in a gal-lop. Conversation is impossible now. Sound waves radiate the room. They bang off the black-light ceiling; they ricochet off cinder walls; they fairly echolocate off the shitty afterthought of a stage. Concus-sive waves batter and beat us to a pulp. Clarence the Smart-Eyed Lion leaves first. He goes outside to fire up a cigarette he bought in *Neverwuz*. I feel a breeze chill my neck and hear loudly, the quiet night outside. Bumbo gets up to take a leak and daub his mouth cor-ners. Marcel goes with him to make sure he does not get shit-kicked. Fizzy and I watch them emerge and then go outside the main exit to be with Clarence. I see blue tail flies around the lights and fire dances beyond the door.

By now the octave is too high and the pain so intense that Fizzy and I must flee. I drain my drink. He slam-dunks his shot and we are out through the in-door. The boys look like a herd of horses as steam rises off their flanks. Marcel says his ears still ring. The Old Boy wore hearing aids and I know the Hearing Aid Reaper comes for me to-night. After three days I still hear Sherwood Forest reverberate in my ears. The cops later bust Smile for being a health hazard.

"Somebody bust you for being an Arse-hole," Bumbo says. "Whose idea was this?"

"Let's go home," Fizzy says for all of us.

Bumbo whistles for the milk wagon but it does not come. We hear *clippy-clops* somewhere in the night but then they fade. Old Gray has left the building.

We pass dollar stores and pharmacies chained together. I have no idea how the Blue Star Restaurant survives but it does survive. The steaks are that good. Nobody has any cigarettes and Meadow-larks are now passé. We cross the familiar grid of the Old Bridge. I gaze down from on high and see the sick belly-white of a Carp carcass pass under our legs. We turn to gaze east. The moon is full over the Bay of Tranquility. A trumpet of light bathes me. I feel it pierce my heart, tickle my spine and exit through my back. I pivot to see it peter out up river while gasps of black water consume all colour and chords.

It is late. We are tired. We wander up from the outskirts to find, Old Eldorado, our Street of Gold. We pass Bryce's. At the front of Old Lady RightBag's house we stop and grow giddy.

"Oh, see Old Lady Rightbag. She is our grade eight teacher. She is very mean. Ouch, ouch, ouch!" says the strap.

"You are not the only pebble on the beach," says the ancient teacher. "Oh, Oh, Oh! Where is your homework?"

"See the day planner. I am going to take the day planner," says Clarence. "I am going to take the day planner at the end of the day. I am going to throw the day planner into the Fishn'Shit."

"Clarence, you Arse! Was that you?" I ask.

"No. It was Suckie. The kid in Joel-the-Hole's class. Remember that expendable dick he invited to Werewolf? Suckie," he repeats solemnly.

I see the Handy Dandy differently now. The Greaseballs and their immolating thumbs are gone. Even though it is late, throngs of boys and girls loiter at the crossroads. They have vials of honey oil and carefully paint their rolling papers brown to look like nicotine stains on hundred-dollar bills and leopard skins.

Clarence decides to stay for a while.

The rest of us stumble into our cow trails and disperse for home. It is another long day. I quietly make a sandwich, have some pop and chips, maybe another sandwich, just a few more chips and go to bed. There are a few honeymoons on the counter, so I munch them too. The stair boards creak in my asbestos house, so I have to straddle them, one at a time, on their very outsides. It is wise not to be heard tonight. Better still, not to be seen. My brother knows the smell.

At the edge of morning, I dream a dream: *Clarence gets rid of his bee collection the hard way.* In the days before apps when boys walk the earth, it is fashionable amongst the scientific to capture and collect bee specimens. There is something about the malevolence of bees that makes it necessary to catch them, bring them up close and see where their stingers really are. The abdomen of a hornet throbs with rage and I can see it spear the glass with its butt. It does its utmost to get Clarence in his other good eye.

Now, it comes to pass that Clarence is over at the Baby Park with a couple of us in tow. The white clover heads are in dainty clusters with just the right mix of lazy afternoon sun and no breeze. We want perfect specimens. It is off limits to stamp a bee with your foot, dent a wing, or twist a thorax. A pickle jar is a perfect tool. Not the small gherkin jars, one of the fat dill jars. Clarence shows me I can still get one hand around it and there is more space inside to observe so long as I soak the label off.

Marcel appears out of nowhere like an explanation mark ("Huh? Oh, Hi Dummy!") and now the three of us, track hornets, yellow jackets, queen bees, honey bees and the evil cousin of the blue tail fly, the indigo mud dauber. The indigo mud dauber is not often seen. When I do see one, I give it a wide birth. It is deep blue, oily, tougher than a hornet and constantly pissed off. Its demonic face in repose makes it an easy date for any bat in town after dusk. Most of us kill a mud dauber if he gets too close.

Clarence the Nerd-Eyed Lion stalks one right now. He studies it for a while. When it lights on the sand, he races in and jams the dill pickle jar over it, tilts it and then claps the lid on, along with a mouthful of grass and clover. His breath is rapid in the thrill of victory. I bring it in close and marvel at its personality; the burr of wings, the mad bash off the glass, the urgency to get out and sting the hell out of Clarence first and then me.

"Seriously, bee, it is Clarence," I say and hook my thumb towards him. "We are just along for the expedition. We just follow orders."

I like to capture a firefly this way but it is important to get a hammer and nail and poke a few holes in the lid so it can breathe. The glow of a firefly is otherworldly, magical, with colours not found on the palate of mortal earth. It is an abomination to keep one too long. A boy would have to be an animal to catch one and not release it immediately. Expendable boys tend to keep them and I am glad when they leave us and move off into their night.

There are no nail punctures on Clarence's lids when he collects bees. In time, the indigo mud dauber quiets. It looks sad. It walks along the seam of the lid, faulters and then drops. Clarence likes to leave it for a day just to be sure. Then he shakes the jar up close to his face to check for any movement. When he is sure, he slips off the lid and dumps the perfect specimen in a larger jar with his full collection.

My pillow feels so cozy. The insides of my eyelids sense the light change. I have a good stretch, all the way from the bottom to the tippy-top. Clarence comes out of his asbestos shingle house and runs towards me up the driveway. He trips, falls but manages to save the jar from smashing. The lid skitters off, turns in circles and waffles to a halt.

"*Buh dee chee chee*," Fizzy says.

"Nice one, Clarence," I say.

Bumbo feels bad and helps Clarence locate all his bees and put them back into the big jar. Clarence counts. He counts again. He asks me to count, because Bumbo is not so good with numbers. We agree one bee is missing. We check species. We agree the missing bee is a Queen bee.

"What the hell," Clarence says. He turns a full 360 degrees.

His face grows white. Unexpectedly, he pulls down his blue corduroy pants. I see his snow-white undies and suddenly feel that all of us are babies really. His pants clump to his feet. There she is! The Queen, with her hairy barbs, alive! Come back from the dead! She makes her way over his knee and onto his thigh. Clarence madly flicks twenty times with his forefinger and thumb but misses the Queen completely. Panic influences aim. I see it.

I feel the burning stab, all of us howl and Clarence cries his face off. He cups his hand over his thigh. Nobody laughs.

Uneasily, I wake up with a vague sense that something is missing in my life. The edge of a dream leaves the oddest feeling.

Somewhere a phone rings and I hear the Old Boy tell me it is Bumbo, and when am I planning to get up? I seem to sleep in more now. Longer if I could.

Snow falls thick, lingers and then collects upon the ground. Bumbo wants to toboggan. By now we tire of the Baby Hill behind *Tanglefoot Acres.* It serves its purpose. Today, we form a caravan, six- and seven-foot toboggans in tow, a couple of saucers and five or six cigarettes. It is a long hike on foot. We walk everywhere now, scruffy, like a pack of dogs filled with the scent of desire. Pinky is the first of us to get a good beard going. Fizzy is next. I try and give up. The snow is thicker now. We slug our way past the Handy Dandy and over the New Bridge. A street curls to the back around the Bowels. We take that and then stair-step up three residential roads to get elevation to the top of a long hill on the southside of *Oncewuz.* Behind the houses, a copse of pine trees stands sullenly. They protest the gravity of a relentless heavy snow.

We ascend a narrow asphalt laneway, protected by ice-coated boughs. A large water tower sits at the base of an afterthought of a wooden stairway. The stairway is made with timber from the creosote plant. Grey rectangles, painted hodgepodge, cover the base of the water tower. I see that "Skid" is back with his graffiti gang, strange hieroglyphics, orange replica penises, and contempt.

"That asshole gives us all a bad name," Fizzy says.

It is par for the course on Mount Pecker. Mount Pecker is not a real mountain but it is real enough. We drag our toboggans up the stairs. The stairs are steep, slippery and we are thankful for the rails. The wind is up and the white clouds of our breath smear into leaden greys flecked with snow at the top. Sammy Champagne's cannon is here. It links our past with our present and for that reason, I have to touch the mighty barrel to ground myself. The cannon is black again. Townies restore it to its former glory. I am sure a guy is hired full time to paint over the wayward spore of youth. Sammy's cannon easily has forty coats on it by now. It is positioned in resolute aim over the Bay of Tranquility, sentinel to the mouth of the river and long before her water mutates into the Fishn'Shit. Because it is there for the taking, we climb the metal grid of the lookout tower to stand upon a platform. *Oncewuz* is obscured by a curtain, but we see ice slowly form along the Bay. The Bay of Tranquility awaits happily the day a micro-town of multi-coloured fishing shanties dot and sprinkle her expanse. Squeak and I pull a nice-size pickerel and a couple of walleyes out of here, last year. Our hands are cold and greasy with fish slime. I smell it like yesterday.

By now we have the shivers. We are careful to descend the tower and easily find the path that runs along the ridgeline of Mount Pecker. I bring up the rear. Oddly, we look noble, like *coureur des bois* who pull their toboggans and go off into the wilderness to trade things of unknown value. I am proud of us. For the most part we keep out of trouble. Not a single soul commits a felony. We are as Innocent as the driven snow.

Fizzy is up ahead. I see him stop and point downwards. We congregate beside him and I see he picks a good spot. Two of us are not so sure, but we talk them into it. A number of corridors run down the steep side of the mount. There appears to be enough room between the trees. The bottom is a mixture of reeds and bramble, enough to stop a six-foot toboggan with ease and well before the stand of evergreens at the foot of the incline.

"I will man up and go first because I am not a baby," Joel-the-Hole announces.

"*Your master's gone a-way,*" I sing. "You are going to die."

I set up my toboggan slightly apart and to his right.

We are not sure, but the key to success is to ride feet first and on our backs. I lay prone and brace my feet against the curl of the toboggan. My butt is so cold, I cannot feel the ribs of the wooden frame and this is a good thing. I grip the ropes along the side while Clarence picks up the back of the toboggan and takes aim. Pinky does the same for Joel-the-Hole. At the count of three we launch footloose and fancy free. I lose sight of Joel-the-Hole. I lose sight of everything. The snow is pristine, so deep that it sprays back and covers my torso and head. The outer rind of danger is on the edge of fun. A tree grazes my arm. I cannot breathe. Panic sets in. I am too scared to use my heels to brake. The decision is made for me when an eight-inch maple brings the toboggan to a complete stop. They say they hear the wood crack from the bottom all the way up to the top. Moaning, I roll off face first into the snow for comfort, convinced my vertebrae shrink and I am now a midget. The wind in the trees is so peaceful. When the shivers set in, I hear voices that unceremoniously, lift me to my feet. Somebody brushes my back right down to the rump. Perpetually, I am accused of faking.

"Jimmy? I've got good news and bad news," Pinky says. The good news is that your face is in tact and you are going to live. The bad news is your toboggan is a write-off. You are in a world of trouble, son."

We break two slats off the frame of the toboggan and belt it to Joel-the-Hole's arm to keep his elbow from bending. It turns out he cleared the bramble and reeds but met the same fate I did with the evergreens.

"We can't take you anywhere," Clarence says and we all laugh.

Like pack mules, we haul Joel-the-Hole back up to the ridgeline. We stamp our feet, wrestle to stay warm and then suddenly, I am alone. No snow falls and I hear the restrained roar of wind, high above, in invisible corridors that define the atmosphere. I drag my feet along the ridgeline to the base of the lookout tower and I hear the bong of my footsteps ascend metal stairs to the observation platform, above. I am surprised to see Fizzy at the top.

"I am coming with you," he says to me.

"Fine by me," I say.

The view from on high is majestic. The air is clear now and no matter where I turn there are panoramas of both meaning and memory. I follow the arc of a cannon ball, high out over the Old Bridge and right down onto the mouth of the Bay of Tranquility. The explosion carries no noise. When the white smoke blows off, I discover the beautiful shapes of our ice shanty town, at intervals like a handful of jacks scattered over a surface of smooth ice. Tiny black curlicues twist over the huts in active use. Snow machines pull travois and men in red hunting caps stand in clusters. As if looking through a microscope, I twist the lens and feel the confined chill of an ice hut seep into my marrow. A Mickey of rye appears and I take my swig. Short fishing rods lean on tripods and the taut line is heavy with anticipation. The only difference between stargazing and fishing is the direction I look. I am made happy by this insight and make a wish that has nothing to do with size or number or bragging rights in shanty town. Small concentric rings form in the hole, there is a tug, another one and by now I have the rod in my hands and can feel the pulse of something living below. I love the tension and I feel the purity of life tingle the palm of my hands. Behold the pickerel. Green and beautiful and defiant. His mouth and gills puff with a synchronicity so indignant, that I chuckle, tenderly comfort him and tell him it is OK. "Don't worry," I think silently. "I will send you back down into the aqueous expanse and see what becomes of you."

His eye rivets me, then inspects. His twists stop their spasms yet the flick and flop that is still in him, forcefully controls my arm. I reach for the pliers, remove the red devil, careful not to tear his mouth. Slowly, I back his tail down through the hole. We take a final reckoning of one another and I release him to gravity. Kiss me, you fool. Like a green bolt and flash of yellow he is gone.

It is time to go and I exit the fishing hut. The fellow beside me tinkers with his tackle.

"Any luck?" he asks.

"Yes" I say. "You should see the one that got away!"

I see he ignores me from my perch on the observation deck. The air is soft on my cheeks and I feel the spring thaw come. Warm water from shore pushes the ice back and one by one I watch the fishing shanties hesitate and then release themselves from this earth. Each hut slips below and flutters like a flat stone to rest on the bottom of the Bay of Tranquility.

An interior sun emerges to shine full bore and illuminate the landscape. It shines directly through my eyes with a clarity so crystalline that I am made to see colours that do not exist. The effect is like a searchlight in broad daylight. I shake my head with my eyes open simply to watch the beams play. When I focus, the entire panorama of *Oncewuz* is before me. The vistas are like still-life photographs in an album but at the same time fluid, living and clicking, like the warm clatter of a projector.

My eyes fall easily on the Holy Trinity and I walk them past Bryce's to the Handy Dandy. The piano chords are vivid and firecrackers blow off with abandon. I peer along the Street of Gold, up past the house with asbestos shingles and my gaze lights upon a boy. He scales a fence to retrieve a ball. He hurls it skyward to catcalls and cacophony. I am glad he does not hurt his nuts.

Mrs. Phil is out by the bike stand. I see she waves and I wave back without moving my arm. I see every pop bottle in every privet hedge along every street in every neighbourhood. The effect is like diamonds twinkling on a living treasure map. The light beholds a gaggle of boys as they run through evergreens, engrossed in play. They sense the light but do not look up to find its source. A bloody t-shirt sits in a garbage can. How lucky they all are to have made it, relatively intact. How lucky they are to be loved. I see the random beauty of friendships discovered. The sun makes their fondness dazzle. The wind shifts and I smell a fragrance, so aromatic it replaces all being. The scent is somewhere between rose petals and sweet pipe tobacco.

I hear the clip-clop of horse hooves to the east and over the old bridge. I cast my beam to find Old Gray. There he is! Marcel Marceau is on the buckboard and gently holds the reins. He waits for Bumbo to complete his delivery. Bumbo is possessed. I see it in the concentration on his face. Delivering milk is his Use. It is what he is good at. It is what he wants to be good at. I love he is so good at it and hug that old arse with my eyes when he wipes his drool off my sleeve. I see that Clarence the Hard-Guy Lion is not on the milk wagon. My light traces first the Handy Dandy, and then the footpath in between houses on the Street of Gold. There are boys there rolling leopard and hundred-dollar-bill skin-me-ups in the shade. A nighthawk swoops by and I track her down and then skyward. Clarence is backlit by clouds amidst a murder of crows. He appears jet black and filled to the brim with knowledge. They all fly too high. I see some falter. Feathers drop. There is nothing I can do for them.

Old Gray whinnies, I turn east and see him face me. Mister Marceau and Bumbo stand on the wagon and wave that exaggerated over-the-head wave we do. I know they leave *Oncewuz* now, to go up along the apple route, around the Bay of Tranquility to the orchards, to dwell among their people: The Boodies, the Wah-Wahs, the Wee-Wees and the Bee Bops. I know I will never see them again. Squeak and Pinky and the rest of the boys all board an airplane. They too, turn in the doorway to wave goodbye.

I hear they all go out to play in the tar sands and make a fortune.

My mind is tired now. The sun is on the wane. The light from my eyes carries mist.

The stately rock of a sailboat cuts through the Old Bridge and over the black gleams of the Fishn'Shit. Prisms of light illuminate this bog of the river. A thousand mudcat troll the silt with a misery so aimless I weep. Somewhere, a spider backs into his cone. I see men tire, commiserate and sip Mickeys in the shade of a tie mill. They pull a little farther into shadows to evade the foolish, untried beam of my eyes. I see they are content. I see they make their way. There is food on their table. There is beer in their fridge. Maybe in time I will settle for something but for now I cannot settle for anything.

My gaze takes me up and around the bend. The river is the Purdy now. The lock roars. The lion waits to be fed. Swarms of blue tail flies buzz the entire dam while every boy in harm's way sings Jimmy Crack Corn at the top of his lungs.

I sing it too. I cannot get it out of my head.

Of course, I find Dug Hill in the mist. A Cherubim, sword aflame, guards the gate. Upon closer look, I see that she is not alone. Thousands of spirits stand vigil in a radiant choir of peace. The oak trees behind Them burst with majesty. The plots are pristine. I envy the tellings of headstones, see flowers and rock borders and every tender gift placed with meaning upon marble. I recognize so many names in Dug Hill, with little to no effort to find them.

I see a family stand by an open grave. Two attendants lower a pine box with pulleys. There is no one else around. I hear the thrum of snare at intervals and the roll carries long in the air. A young man reads from a book, tears the page clean out and I watch it flutter and disappear down a hole. I see the family hug and leave. A backhoe pours in dirt and the attendant shovels the excess in a way that even, from a distance looks efficient. The mound rises slightly, somehow moist and puffy, like a scar waiting to fade and settle into skin. Three corner stones are set in place.

The light wavers now. Nightfall changes all colour into warm reds and purples. It is not unpleasant. The observation tower is a silhouette. *Oncewuz* is a silhouette and I am free to leave.

"C'mon, Fizzy," I say. "Let's get out of here."

Chord ii
(and I don't care)

Chord ii
(and I don't care)

"Your problem, Jimmy," Fizzy says to me, "is that you got good at something you did not set out to do."

"Who dies and makes you the authority on it?" I ask Fizzy. "Can I buy you another smash or are you good?"

"Sure, I'll sign on for another."

"He wants mix in it this time," I tell Sammy behind the bar.

"*Buh dee chee chee,*" we say to the clink of glass.

"Did I ever tell you the parable of the Do-Gooder Inn, Fizzy?

"A noble fella walks down the tarmac and sees this other guy lie in a ditch. He is bloody, beaten to a pulp and drags himself under the soft red leaves of a sumac bush to lick his wounds. The noble fella stops, bandages his carcass and hauls his sorry arse into an Inn. He gives the Innkeeper some money for food and lodging and leaves. Repeat to infinity. Not just for the guys but for girls too, whole families, babies, young people and all that. At a certain point the old Bleeding-Heart tires of the cycle, leaves the road and heads off into a forest. I always wonder where he goes for peace and quiet so I track him. I wonder if he smokes or sips rye like I do. Deep in the forest, the trees part to reveal a farm and the farm leads directly over a knoll to the steps of the Do-Gooder Inn. I am right behind him when he goes in. He sidles up to the bar and sure enough, I watch him order a smash, straight up, no mix. I have what he has. The bar is a sea of ordinary heroes living ordinary dreams. Somebody puts on Link Wray and the Wraymen and the sound is so good inside, I forgive him. I am compelled to empathy in this space. We all are. I behold this symphony of laughter and good will, hear the repetitive clink of glass and eat as many sauerkraut hotdogs as I desire. We take turns behind the bar to serve one another. I barely serve two drinks in a row before someone else volunteers to pour. Relieved of my duty, I go out to buss tables and take orders. I chance upon two Samaritans from the east. I sense only the sound of intense listening between us.

"'I'll buy you a drink,' I tell them.

"'No, I'll buy you,' the Samaritan on the right says.

"'And the other Jimmy Crack Corn, it is my round, Bub,' the Samaritan on the left counters. His eyes are kind but intense.

"A third guy comes up and offers to buy all three of us a shot.

"'No, it's all good, I got this one, Bud,' I insist.

"Suddenly, there is thunder and lighting, the bar splits open and the place is bedlam. I can't find enough guys to hit and I'm sure I went down three times.

"Tables go over, bottles break and before I know it, we are all on the floor, moaning. I look up, my sight clears and I see a Cherubim. Link Wray still warps inside my head. It is not that unpleasant. When I gaze up again, I see the Cherubim divide to become five angels. Each one ministers to us at intervals, upon the floor.

"'Jimmy! You are a bleeder!' a girl-angel says, when she daubs my cut. Her touch is so tender I start to cry. The tears have nothing to do with the nick under my eyebrow."

"If you tell me you are wearing your best t-shirt, I am going to hit you," Fizzy interrupts.

"Don't look in your top dresser drawer at least for a week, Chum," I tell him.

"Anyway, the girl-angel lifts me unceremoniously to my feet and dusts me off. She stuffs money in my pocket and hauls me to another Inn to mend. The Cherubim pay the Innkeeper enough for the weekend and then I am free to go."

"The cycle never stops, does it?" Fizzy says, presciently.

"No, it does not," I tell him.

"Did I ever tell you I was in a strip joint and a wedding on the same day?" Fizzy asks out of the blue.

"Why the hell do you do that?" I ask.

"Have to run an experiment," he says matter-of-factly. "It is a long month and I am tired. Tired of the urban wars. See too much, I guess. All my circuits blow and I have to get my innocence back is the crazy way to tell it. So, I am in this club and I tell you this babe is on stage in a flimsy dress. She dances like she rolls in clover, nice hips and all that. At the refrain, "ugh, ugh, ugh," she lifts up the hem of her skirt three times and I see the prettiest Delta-P on this planet. 'Do it again' we yell and she does, "ugh, ugh, ugh." A Delta-P is what happens up at the Purdy when a diver goes in to inspect for leaks in the lock. Lower a sandbag on a rope and check for the suction. If I don't inspect first and dive straight in, I get sucked right into the void and nobody will get me out. Over. Done like dinner."

"Fizzy, I didn't know you were a Flying Frogman in *Oncewuz*," I say.

"I was," Fizzy says. "Love it like breathing, but let it go. I was good at it too and the other I don't care.

"So anyway, I propose in my loins to the gal, she declines and then I go to church. The bride is radiant. What I see exist between the eyes of the two of them, I cannot describe. All lust is barred at the door. I see a love so tangible. I feel it consume me to the marrow and beyond, Jimmy. I see the simple promise of life itself. Within my grasp. I hold it for a while and then let it go, like those fireflies we capture and release.

"Suddenly, I feel ancient. It is like a wind passes through me with no quality, no chill, no warmth but a presence. Maybe truth alone does not have temperature. I wonder about that. If there is a speech that silently exists between our eyes, it is possible that life is love and love is giving and all the rest is just journey and trappings and *go-for's* and *go-to's* and *git-er-duns*.

"The afternoon passes gently and I find myself at a reception table across from Davie, a man who is a pal of the Old Boy. Like I say, the Old Boy is dead by now, but I like to sit with this guy. I listen and ask questions. I treat him with respect. He is deaf like us. Screws his hearing as an artillery gunner, during the war. After that, he works in construction. One of the important guys in the white hats that works out the logistics: how many bulldozers, back hoes and dump trucks to have on site and all that. Big boy stuff in a sandbox of epic proportion.

"I can tell he likes to talk about it and by now I have my eye on the door to see if anybody goes out for a smoke. No one goes so I am stuck. I sip a little wine, roll up my sleeves, spread my elbows like a triangle and rest my chin on my hands."

"'What do you do for a living?' Davie asks me.

"'I am a baby snatcher,' I tell him. 'Help kids and all that stuff.'

"His *meathooks* are big as steaks and the only thing he thinks to say is, and I quote: 'What do you want to be a Do-Gooder for?'"

"Fizzy!" I say. "What a royal Arse! Do you slug him?"

"No, like I say he is a friend of the Old Boy. It is all I can do, though, not to slap the white helmet off his bus-depot head and give him a mouth full of bloody chicklets. Then he looks at my ring finger. 'Congratulations,' he says out of the blue.

"'I am not a Mason, Davie,' I tell him. 'This is my father's. He lets me spin it when I sit on his lap and we watch *Gunsmoke*.'

"'You should take the ring off,' he says, not listening.

"'Well you should fuck off,' I tell him. I get up and leave."

"Whups," I say to Fizzy, tenderly.

"Ya, I already stank of buffalo robe and pemmican so I got the hell out of that church gymnasium, pay my respects to the bride and groom and go home. End of field experiment."

"Buy me another drink," Fizzy says.

"I drink to forget," I tell him.

"Forget what?"

"You nagging me."

"*Buh dee chee chee.*"

"What did you do about the corner stone? Did you get up to Dug Hill?"

"It is still on my mind, Fizzy."

"Sammy! Two more smashes please. One for me, and one for this Ape."

I am at a crossroads again but there is not a Soul around. Not a single Greaseball immolates his thumb. Pop bottles have no currency and firecrackers are banned now. Some arse probably put an eye out, and thereby fulfills the great parental prophesy to spoil today's future for tomorrow's children. Boys no longer walk the earth but it is in the days well before apps.

I sail a northerly course and come upon two young men from *Neverwuz*. They are flat broke like me and in search of part-time work. It is the days of thicker school books and we no longer use crayons, bored to tears with our lot.

"Oh Jimmy! If you don't know what to do, do something and see what happens" is the Old Girl's "yogi bear" advice and exasperation.

Mingus and Tex encourage me to come south with them to Cherry Street. They have a weekend job and shuffle mufflers in the city. The pay is over three dollars. "It is a good, steady gig, Jimmy," they tell me and for a moment I am tempted to run with them. I meet a girl at the same time who works on a project to teach children how to do their math better. Some of them hear funny and some of them don't talk right. All of them share the roller-coaster misery of being good at failing. The project needs another hired hand.

"Come with me, Jimmy!" she beckons all ripe and come hither, moist like a mermaid upon a rock. The air is expectant. It wonders what I will do. When the screech of seagulls breaks open the stillness, I make my decision.

She is a girl, after all. Her job pays a quarter more an hour and I get paid to learn the program before I even meet Stinky. I bring Fizzy with me and together we change direction, turn east like wise men, but with as much nobility as a pair of carp. Change at the crossroads is that random. And with the change, I have enough cigarettes, enough rye and enough Philly cheese steaks to continue to collect my A's and build a reputation. My wings are fulsome in their feathers and flow well off the back of my arms. I turn, crick my neck and gaze at a sun I never really notice before. I feel its warmth on my face, right through my face into my heart and lungs and beyond that to a deeper anatomy of form. "I can fly," I declare to Fizzy.

In a moment, I forget when, I pair with little Stinky. He looks alright to me and try as I might, I cannot see what his problem is. Once a week, week upon week, we use the secret method I am paid to learn. Stinky does his best. He enjoys the attention but both of us feel antsy to play after the lesson.

I meet Tex and Mingus at the campus pub and we compare notes over sauerkraut dogs or ham and grilled cheese if it is a Tuesday. They seem happy with the mufflers. There are weekends where I wish I was with them on Cherry Street. I am not sure why I always sit alone and face them together in the booth. It is well before my hearing is shot, but I still miss half of what they laugh about. It is all too subtle to notice.

On Monday, I am back with Stinky. There are always ten minutes left at the end of our session, now. Sometimes he likes to draw so we draw. Sometimes he brings in some Play-Doh from class and we roll snakes or build lions. We go outside when the weather is nice and race in opposite directions to be the first back at the front door of the school. I rule out shingle tag, but show him how to collect leaves and we make a little book. I cannot believe I get three dollars and fifty cents an hour to do this. I buy him a set of coloured pencils. He spirits them away with a cute little grin. Once when I come to get him, I see his pictures proudly fly like flags over the cloak room and over the blackboard. I hear he collects some A's and word gets back to me that he cleans up in math now. I don't even know what to think but I am happy the little Ape is happy. At the end of the term, we part ways, with little fanfare, like brothers on separate errands. I tell Tex and Mingus one Friday night that I miss the kid. They laugh and tell me I am a *softee.*

"Actually, I really like him," Fizzy tells me.

Fizzy and I continue to head east on foot. The crossroad is well behind us and disappears in the distance. It is like looking up and seeing my eyes in a rear-view mirror before my gaze shifts. A Maverick appears and then morphs into a Milk Wagon. Bumbo is long gone but Old Gray is not, so we hop on. It is good to see him again and I brush away the blue tail flies around his head with a hickory broom. Tex and Mingus are somehow in the back so I turn to say hello. At the edge of the treeline I sense that I am followed. Out of the corner of my eye, I spy with my little eye, a Werewolf. He looks over his shoulder and then disappears into the forest. Through the spaces, at intervals I see him walk parallel to the road and the effect is like a processional. Step by step to the rumble of snare drum.

"Do you see that?" I ask Fizzy.

"Hear what?" he says.

"Never mind," I say. I am distracted and realize I am far enough down the road that it is time to pick. The great choosing is always so indifferent. It is like the locks and roaring lion of the Purdy. The water decides to either eat you or let you have fun in it. We all do something, everybody does and what does it really matter what we do? It is Purdy random after all. The jig is up. Time waits only so long and then it is replaced by an interior clock of desire, a yearning so deep, a ticking so loud that a decision must be made if only to relieve the tension and keep the cogs from stripping. No more firemen. No more forest ranger. No more writer. No more oceanographer and all the Scuba gear is in the closet. Fizzy is so bad at science and his marks suck. Visions of his future appear. They shimmer like an oasis in the desert. Fizzy squints and says he sees a jazz quartet play up ahead. There is a marquee atop a city bar. I strain to hear the squawk and screech of Eric Dolphy's bass clarinet. A piano solos, the drummer and upright bass keep time. Dat, dat, dat and datly-dat on the snare of joy. It is wild and free and I love it. The musicians look at each other, laugh and then disappear. A phantom jet streaks overhead and startles Old Gray. I see a glint of light on a cannister of napalm tumble end over end and in the distance the entire oasis and half a city is taken out in a ball of orange and black. I want to say to Fizzy that the colour reminds me of a scoop of Tiger ice cream at Bryce's but to be honest, it looks nothing like that at all.

Mingus is the first to understand and then Tex.

"Welcome to the urban wars," they say prophetically.

"Hell no, I won't go," Fizzy protests.

"And the other Jimmy Crack Corn," I tell him. "If I go, you go."

I click my tongue and goad Old Gray into the flames.

I am not yet worthy to enter the Charred City so I have to learn the real lessons before I gain access. I realize that I am in a sweat-lodge probed by spirits greater than my own. We chance upon a pool not unlike the biblical pool of Bethsaida. This pool is a swimming pool and I hear the echo of a whistle and the amplified colour of sound ripple like waves across the ceiling. The humidity makes me cozy and the smell of chlorine scrunches my nose and my nostrils flare. The water is up to my waist, so warm and steam-y. Fizzy and I guide a wheelchair down a ramp into the brine. The wheelchair, hard, resolute, unbuoyant rests at chest level and I pull the lever and feel the brake catch. Tenderly, we unstrap the straps. A body gently rises. There is a screech of delight, guttural, almost animal-sounding. It is released from a depth that makes my eyes tear. There is nothing in the chord I recognize. I have no reference point. It is not the tintinnabulation of my school yard. Later, I realize it is the sound of *Neverwuz*. I still hear it and when I hear it, I feel tepid pool-water on my chest, rise up past my nipples, under my outstretched chin and I wonder if I will drown.

The resurrection begins and like two damn Cherubim, Fizzy and I glide the boy out of the confines of his chair. Someone pulls the contraption back up the ramp. I am glad. It does not belong in this atmosphere and in fact it is an offense. I gently push the boy's legs, shift along his length to place my hand under his neck and watch real Cherubim tenderly float him to the surface. My cheek is right beside his face. His delight is my delight. I am so close, I do not know where his smile ends and my smile begins. His laughter is repetitive, like little squawks of sound that bite the air and echo loudly. His breath is not so good to smell and I don't care. His master's gone away and while he is away, the kid just has me and I just have him. I wonder when the last time I felt the pure happiness his entire body feels right now, within the forever of one moment. He freaking shivers with glee. The last time I shiver with glee is up at the freaking Purdy. I share the elemental moment with the boy and together we fly in the aqueous space until a voice whispers it is time to soar back to the ramp. His chair is in the water. I duck my head and see the belts forlorn in their suspension like octopus's arms that wait symmetrically to squish. Fizzy and I guide the boy along the surface and I turn him to face out. I place my hand on his back, and push down on his knees. Soon gravity arrests him. His sentence shocks me. He is strapped down and fettered. The chair is part of his body, again. I watch him back slowly up the ramp to disappear. He is happy. I pivot, push off and light a cigarette.

Outside a brown square Naugahyde building with ten-foot windows, like an old school on the outskirts of a charred city, I stand with five novitiates. As if on tour, we march past an admissions desk. I am not sure if the nurse smiles. I am self-conscious and my full gaze turns inward to illuminate my insecurity, my embarrassment and my fear. I do see the attendants in their gray coveralls. I can relate to them. They are everywhere and walk the slow-walk not meant to get anywhere too soon. For the life of me, they look like union men, standing in the shade of railroad ties, in the north yard of the creosote plant on the bank of the FishnShit. I adjust to the inner light and the atmosphere is fluid. The eyes of the attendants all look like fish eyes. Bulbous and moist. Uncomfortably touched by oxygen. The flick and flop is barely in them. It is as if they are all gasping on the bank of a river, her water so temptingly close. They are spasmodic and hurl themselves, inch by grass-y inch to the water at five o'clock.

Single file I walk up stairs with the novitiates. I try not to touch the handrails. The light is opaque and the air smells like the dirt has only been shifted by ammonia and floor wax. We come to a ward. A bolt is moved and we enter. I am in a large space known as a day room. Our guide chats with the attendants. They are used to the intrusion and their smiles and head-nods, are the complete antithesis of welcome. "O geezis, the Do-Gooders are here," I see them shrug with a disinterest so careless my fist balls. The citizens of the day room share the same indifference. I don't feel human. I see variation upon variation of images here. It is like the brittle refraction of a haunted house mirror when greasy carnies come to *Oncewuz,* in the rain. Good God, they all look like Bumbo. I think the lesson is to say I witness a micro-cephalic, a hydro-cephalic, can stand the smell of feces and the look of snot and that masturbation is "self-stimming." It is really hard to know for there is no de-brief after five o'clock and I walk out to the Maverick in shock, pissed off to the exponent blue and the other *I don't care.* I murder my cigarette in a parking lot in *Neverwuz.*

"Nobody comes to see them," the attendant says, as he locks the ward.

"Fuck the blue tail fly," I say to Fizzy. "Get me out of here."

"Jimmy! You're a bleeder!" he laughs.

"And you are an arse," I tell him.

The road takes Fizzy and I and whomever else I bring to a cluster of buildings that exude science and learning in an exact ratio and proportion of a reputation. I make the choice, and because I make the choice I am in vague control of my action. It is the beginning of a power yet to be harnessed. Fizzy and I feel like we are in a beehive only it is wide, open and well lit. There is nothing random about this space. I sense a synchronicity of purpose: no one action is random, no one action is of itself. I sense the gray, paper-y boundaries but do not see them from where I stand. What I do see, is drones and worker bees, several Queens and each with an intrinsic instinct of why they do what they do. They know why they are what they are. I wonder if they all chose their lot or got good at something they did not choose to do. There is no time to ask, for it is understood that Fizzy and I are to be instructed. We enter a small sub-chamber and I am surprised to see Tex and Mingus are present. Fizzy and I sidle up beside them and the Samsonite chair feels cold on my butt. We lean into one another, climb over top and around, careful not to step on one another's wings and Mingus whispers that this is a mud-dauber free zone. The property of laughter is to bond and my heart rate goes down. For some stupid reason, I notice I tuck my hands underneath my thighs. I remove them, nudge Fizzy and we cross our arms, slouch back and go for the indifferent intelligent look. Two instructor wasps come into the room and give the four of us the once-over. I see by their grins that they perceive that we actually know nothing. *(The Old Boy used to mock himself and say: "Jimmy, I taught you everything I know and still you don't know nothing!")* There is a freedom to their gift but only because of the smile in their eyes. They proceed to recircuit our wires and teach us how to be bees. It is not unpleasant. There is an ozone stink when some of Fizzy's wires short and sputter, and I learn to tear them out like a fistful of hair. After a time, I feel my pitch change. My hum sounds different. So do Mingus's and Tex's but I can tell Fizzy is balking it a bit.

On Tuesday, Fizzy goes first. He sits in a room with a wasp and a man and a woman. The wasp leaves Fizzy with the couple to join me behind a one-way mirror. I volunteer to run the camera console and I behold the proceedings in split screen, quarter screen and marvel at the microscope effect of 10X, 100X and 1000X on the human face.

Humanity is magnified then, in all its profound colour. I see anger form in the corner of eyes, see hatred burst forth in the quiver of a lower lip. His tears glisten so bright, I rub my own eyes behind the mirror. For a moment, I see love hover between them, suspend, decide and then dart away. I see love leave. I take my eyes off the console, look thru the one-way mirror and gaze real-time at the couple. Her arms cross. He says something hurtful and turns to look at Fizzy.

Fizzy looks like a matinee idol. The old arse is doing great right up until she says: "When he kisses me, he leaves too much spit in my mouth."

"*Buh dee chee chee,*" he says.

The wasp leaves me to join Fizzy on the real side of the mirror and save the day. She does save the day. I know because I got it on film. Later, Fizzy, Tex, Mingus and I sit on Samsonite chairs in the sub-chamber to process the episode. I notice three of us sit on our hands and have our heads down. We are gentle with Fizzy. We do not give him the gears. There but for the grace of Jimmy Crack Corn go I. Fizzy sits up straight. He listens hard. Before my eyes, I observe him transform into a baby worker bee. The learning is that acute, and all the rest is nonsense. At five o'clock we exit the hive and stand outside to share a smoke.

"My girlfriend is across the pond," Fizzy says in the parking lot by the Maverick.

"We have this arrangement where we pick a day and a time. I am in a phone booth here. She is in a call box there. At the moment of our choosing, my phone rings. I pick it up and tell the operator in an efficient voice that, yes, I will accept a collect call. Dutifully, the overseas operator patches us through. For the first minute, we talk serious and the other, 'yes honey, your mother is fine,' but after that, we get all love-y and yak our faces off for an hour. We can go longer but I don't want us to get busted."

"Does she kiss pretty good, Fizzy?"

"Damn right," he says. "It is the springtime of youth and I am not a Greaseball."

In the time of new shoots and wild flowers, when Jack-in-the-pulpits give testimony from the heart of the forest floor, when the light changes and warms, some of the reputation of the building rubs off on us. I park, enter the hive and know exactly what my collective purpose is; in fact, I Jimmy-the-Bleeder am almost a worker bee, full-fledged.

Certain icons appear after the crossroads and in my case, it takes the form of six plastic dinosaurs. They are soft and you can move their necks and feet and get some life out of them. A green tyrannosaurus rex in full roar replete with useless little forearms; a stegosaurus, a triceratops, one of those armoured fellas with the club tail and spikes, the one that always appears in cheesy B movies with a dorsal fin that looks like a sail and I forget the last one. They wait for me in a little play room with a mirror and then a boy like Stinky comes through the door. I can tell he wants to eat me. He circles the room. When he slips out of sight, behind my back, the hair on my neck tingles, but soon he presents himself in plain sight. He sees that I sit on the floor and I think this throws him off. He gets to look down on me and I can tell he likes the novelty of that. I ignore him and line up the dinosaurs. He kicks them over with his foot.

"It is the end of the world," I say. "Volcanoes are everywhere. Can we revive them?" I stand them up, the tyrannosaurus in the lead. Stinky kicks them over, again.

"Oh no!" I say. "The meteorites are here. The dinosaurs will all perish! Who can help them?"

It goes like this, about six or seven times, I guess, and soon Stinky sits across from me. The dinosaurs are safe between us in a little harbour of space.

"Hi Stinky," I am scripted to say. "These toys are for you to play with. The only rules are you have to treat them respectfully, you can't hurt me and you can't hurt yourself. You can use these dinosaurs to play the way you need to. They may help how you feel. We will be together for forty-five minutes and I will let you know well before our time is up.

When our time is up, I am exhausted. Fizzy is too. Stinky asks to take a dinosaur. I say, "No, Stinky, you can't but they will wait for you next week at the same time. I will look forward to seeing you and wonder what the dinosaurs will want to say." Later, in an office with a million books a Queen Bee interprets what the dinosaurs tell me. The cards and marbles of *Oncewuz* don't speak to me like this. I meet a mommy dinosaur and a daddy dinosaur and a baby brother dinosaur. The other three sibling dinosaurs have their *doinks* touched and get smacked around. They no longer live at home. The armoured fella with the clubbed tail and spikes gets it the worst. He is very mad and hurts the baby dinosaur sometimes.

"Jimmy," Fizzy says to me one morning, "I am not ready to settle down. I need to go across the pond and make my fortune."

"I'll go with you," I say. "The Old Boy is all over the world during the war as an airman." The nighthawk does not fall far from the nest and when he does fall, the wind comes up from below. His naturally bent wings feel their fullness and find loft. It is a beautiful thing to eat your own June bugs. "Besides," I say. "My brother roams over there and it is time to get a good look at him.

I rub Old Gray between his ears on the soft of his noble head. When I look into the dark well of his eye, I see myself polish the Maverick. I get it ready for sale, noting Fizzy and I have to liquidate. I get rid of everything that is not nailed down in order to make my fortune in the New World. The jump start to success is front money.

It is the beginning of August and I work with Pete. We cut lawns around apartments in the outskirts of *Neverwuz*. Pete and I get along. I tell him I am going across the Pond soon and I need to unload my car.

"How much you want for it?" he asks me while we sip a shot of rye.

"Five hundred bucks," I say. "I need the dough for plane fare and to get started.

"I'll buy it off you," he says and we toast like men.

It is now the exact end of August and I have today and tomorrow to finish up work. I stow away the trimmers and gas cans in the pick-up truck. Pete comes up to me and I expect to settle with him.

"I can't afford five hundred dollars," he says out of the blue. I can tell he is a rat because he looks at me with a little shit-face grin.

"What a rodent," Fizzy says to me on the plane. "How much did you get for it?"

"Two-twenty and the other Jimmy Crack Corn."

"*Buh dee chee chee,*" he says.

Both of us grow quiet now. I turn to look out the oval portal. We are above the clouds. The nose of the plane angles downward, our ears pop and I glimpse a patchwork of rectangles between wisps of air. The sentimental hesitation that leaving brings tugs my heart. Fizzy says something about Bumbo and Clarence the Drug-Addled Lion but I miss it in the hiss of cabin air. Over the intercom, the pilot welcomes us to the other side of the Pond. He hopes we packed our brollies.

Fizzy and I find my brother at the Sun. He recommends the Shepherds' Neam and buys Fizzy and I a pint. We stand and cradle it beside blokes and mates and merriment. I notice how bright the pub is. It is not dark n' dirty like the Sherwood and my brother reminds me that Neam is a major food group.

The three of us occupy a small closet that fits two pallets end to end. On the pallets go a mattress of chesterfield pillows that are in good nick. We pull them from the dumpster down the street. There is space for a small stool and a table to hold our ashtray. A rod at the end gathers our clothes but I did not bring much. The overall effect makes me lonely, but home is home, after all, even though it takes time to grow sweet. There is a small working fireplace, the power is on and we have the only bathtub and hot water in the Angel Coop. In order to take a good bath, I put 10p coins in a box and hear them trickle down somewhere to release water that is questionably hot. It is all a matter of degrees. Fizzy and I constantly make change when the companions in our collective stop by to tidy up.

"Oye! Can you break a quid, Jimmy?"

Our cigarette supply grows to mammoth proportion and like pints, subs in for food at constant intervals.

At a certain point of distress, Fizzy suggests we look for pop bottles to supplement our dwindling income but I decline. The Old Boy would not stoop so low. In the days before apps, there are newspapers and a mail system that comes twice a day. One paper is devoted to Do-Gooder jobs and like pickerel in the Bay of Tranquility, the nibbles start, the line bobs and sure enough I haul one in.

Yesterday, Fizzy walks down the street and a police cruiser pulls up beside him. The bobbies look him over, grin and ask if he would like to be in a police parade.

"They tell me there is four quid in it, if I volunteer," he says.

"So, I get in the cruiser and they take me to a station. There is a lounge there and they ask me to stand shoulder width apart, beside eight blokes. We all have a mustache and it is frightening how three of the guys in line actually look like me.

"Matter of fact, the rest of them look like you, Jimmy!"

"Fizzy, you are a complete arse," I say.

"I know, because I finally figure out what is going on. A woman comes in with a female bobby. There is a sick, yellow bruise around her eye socket. Look straight ahead they tell us. One by one, the women stops, looks, looks again and moves down the line. When she gets to me, I already know I'm guilty and going to be hung and then deported. It is the oddest feeling to feel like a man who commits a crime he did not do. I'm not saying I want to take one for the team, but I want them to get the guy as bad as she does. She gets to the end of the line and disappears. A bobby with a mustache calls me and gives me my four quid. A cruiser returns me to the exact spot they pick me up, like it never happens."

At the end of a noble road lies World's End Estate and a little Do-Gooder club called Flashpoint. Aptly named as the ground zero point when the bomb drops.

I teach the entire population a game Stinky taught me. Get two paper clips and a strip of paper about an inch wide and eight inches long. Fold it into a S shape. Put a clip on the inside of each loop. Make up a story about two lost friends. They try to find each other. Say *clip-clop, clip-drop* and tug the strips out like a party cracker. The paper clips fly into the air and land coupled together, forever friends even though they may never see one another again.

"Fizzy, we cut the strips and tape on the paper clips and send a set out to every parent in those high-rises. Vandalism decreases by 15 percent, nobody incessantly pushes all the elevator buttons and there are zero complaints about urchin-gob off the balcony."

"There comes a time when a young arse gets it out of his system," I tell my brother on the last night at the Sun. The Neam is clear and hoppy. "Yes, I go home penniless but it is plain to see I am a rich man."

"What about your girlfriend?" he asks me tenderly.

"And the other *'clip-clop, clip-drop,'*" I tell him because I am sad.

There is ascension, a levelling off, a testing of wings, the descent to earth and when I return to *Neverwuz*, Fizzy and I are met at the airport by Old Gray.

Call me Icarus.

Fizzy and I hop on, with Fizzy at the buckboard. We *clip clop* east and come to rest at the gates of the Charred City. The blue tail fly bites Old Gray on the haunch. He rears up and half his load of milk bottles slide off the back of the milk wagon to smash upon the ground. It is a godawful mess and when I look up Old Gray is gone and so is Fizzy. I suppose he goes back to the Bay of Tranquility to spend the rest of his days ice fishing and playing euchre. I miss him dearly but he is a forever friend who touches me indelibly. I promise to visit him in the privacy of my own mind. We have a good chat, a good cry and a last hug.

I am in spirit form and I am alone. I am also flat broke and to the point: *If I don't know what to do, do something!*

Begin at the beginning. I call up a friend in the west end and she and her fella can put me up until I get on my feet. It takes about four weeks to process me and a welfare fella from the Samaritan tribes drops by the apartment to assess my state. Better still, he leaves me with my cheque. He sees I am serious about the Do-Gooder life. I am a good risk, in other words and soon, I have enough cigarettes, enough food and enough wherewithal to find my own dog-hole closer to the centre of the Charred City. I reside near the holy trinity of a Bic-disposable life: a laundromat, a 24-hour donut shop and a variety store. The variety store is nothing like Phil's, nothing like Bryce's but perhaps a bit like the Handy Dandy. Street-rats smoke weed, replace Greaseballs and their immolation of thumbs. A constant stream of fellas buy condoms, adult videos, bags of chips and the latest in glassware bong. I haul a jar of peanut butter and a loaf of white bread out of there enough times to be considered a regular. My Landing Zone is a peanut brittle triangle about the size of the Baby Park. I set my claymore mines and square the delta away.

Early, during the morning of the seventh day, I throw in a load of undies next store. The donuts are right out of the oven after the witching hour and I particularly like a warm honey cruller, chased by black coffee, no butch.

I return to the laundromat and transfer my dainties to the dry cycle. I have a sensation that I am not alone and there is an odour now in the air like wet fur. I look down the aisle and there at the back, under the penumbra of a fluorescent light, at the long table, a Werewolf folds clothes. He has that Lon Chaney-thing going on. An oversized white shirt open at the chest with two buttons missing. An elbow is burst at the seams. Half his shirt is tucked in over a pair of khaki pants cinched at the waist with a piece of rope. His knees are dirty and I see he is a shoeless Joe. It is not a bad look on him.

I nod. He nods. The dryer cycle finishes and I load my whites into a green garbage bag and leave. The sun rises and takes its immediate place in the morning to herd men and woman along the variable paths of their commute. At 9:05 my phone rings. I accept an invite into the heart of the Charred City to interview as a Point Man with a Baby Snatcher Unit. They like what I do with the Stinky's of World's End Estate and I get the job. Not a single one of us hopes to get this job during the time I train with wasps. We know enough to steer clear of it. But in fact, probably sixty percent of us sign on for the Urban Wars. After all, they take frightened women and men with zero experience, pay more than three-fifty an hour, the turnover is high and the other so what? There are a thousand reasons not to sign on and one to accept, so I accept.

On the morning of the next day, I report for duty. I meet with human resources, sign my induction papers and I am drummed up stairs to meet my Wasp and the rest of my unit. They are young like me, most of them, with a few veterans thrown into the mix. To a soul, each of them smiles the same smile. It is not a mean smile at all, but one filled with a mixture of sorrow and compassion. There is only a hint of skepticism that I will last. I smile back and again, to a soul, I sense each of them translate the literacy of my unease. "You are right," the corners of my mouth say: "I have no idea what I get myself into and I know enough to shut up, listen and learn." I am introduced to my partner. He shows me my cubicle and my phone and I get the crash-course.

"We cover everything east of the Big Street to the Park. Everything above the lake, north to below the River. On Monday, Wednesday and half of Friday you are on phones, while I am out. On the other days, you are out in the Charred City investigating while I cover phones. Transfer a case after twenty-one days and fight to make sure they let you; otherwise, your caseload will bottle up and you will go crazy."

"Noting same with thanks," I tell him in the shorthand of fear.

I spend the rest of the day on light duty, meet the unit to understand what they do and what I do, read over some files and smoke too many cigarettes.

The light changes, the office grows quiet and I sit at my desk, almost scared to leave because if I leave, I might not come back tomorrow. In my hand I hold a small orange laminated card. I thumb it over and over. It does not have my picture on it. Only my name with signature on the back to prove it is me, the name of my Do-Gooder Unit and my title: Cradle Robber.

"Werewolf! Werewolf!" I say to rally my spirit, get up and leave.

Around the corner is a pub that does not serve Neam. Lon Chaney waits for me and I take the last chair at the bar.

"Lon?" I confess. "Here it is: What am I doing? I don't babysit, never held an infant and barely kiss a girl. I might not be the right fella for this job."

"Jimmy," he says. "It is noble work and you are a born bleeder, you arse. Think of it as Shingle Tag, only you are the shingle."

It is my half of Friday, the afternoon part, and I am out in the northeast quadrant of the Charred City. There are a series of high rises, not unlike the Place of Four Fingers. The buildings are an afterthought to safety. They fill with a gumbo of nooks and crannies, dark spaces and corridors that connect the smell of urine with nicotine. A call comes in and I sign out the Chevelle and leave it a street over. Someone neglects a baby. It is the third call about same. "If somebody does not do something, there is going to be hell to pay," the caller accuses me over the phone. "What good are you people, anyway?"

He likes to drink, she likes to yell, and nobody sees the baby for a few days. I check records and sure enough there are two calls, recorded. The case is opened and closed at point.

A radio fades when I tap on the door. The door opens and stops at the chain. A woman asks me what I want, leaves and then I see a man's face through the crack. I tell him somebody from the community worries about their baby. I ask the baby's name and tell them my sister's baby is Tina too. I don't have a sister and I have no idea how I come up with the line but it works. I tell them it would be great to meet and chat with them. If there are other calls, then you know me and I know Tina. The chain rattles, the door opens and I walk in. The place is relatively clean. The usual small kitchenette, a living room and TV, hallway to one bedroom, bathroom off the side. I smell the cloying stink of steamed broccoli. There is a twelve-pack under the table and four are empty. It is just information and I compare that information with the fact that there is a twenty-four in the cupboard back at my apartment. They seem nice enough so we sit at the table and get to know one another. I decline a cigarette. I see the corner of Little Tina's crib in the living room. When we are comfortable with one another, there is no rush, I ask to meet Tina. There she is. We all smell her diaper and without prompting, the mother lifts Tina out and places her on a bassinette. Tina smiles and so does the Mom. When the tapes rip free and the diaper cups off, heavy with the scent of urine, I see that Tina's crotch and bum are on fire, messy and covered in sores. My heart races and I make a show of talking calmer. I need time. I need time to think. This must be neglect, I hear myself think. My first case. At the point where I am about to open my wallet and produce my tiny orange baby snatcher card without a picture, I somehow think to call for back up. I ask to use their phone. I phone the office and pray like hell that the Homemaker is in. Miraculously she is. Her job, is to help a family with housekeeping, routines and baby care and when I describe what I see, she says it sounds like a nasty case of diaper rash.

"I will be out in half and hour and don't do anything till I get there," she orders.

True to form she arrives and I let her in. I introduce her to the family and to Tina. Sarah has that old Mom-thing going and even I feel comfortable with her ease with the couple, the baby and with me. Out comes the zinc oxide and the diagnosis of diaper rash. Sarah, leaves a can for the Mom and agrees to come back in two days for tea, chat and progress.

Outside, Sarah is gentle with me and I love her for it. She knows I am poised to strike and feel all the more foolish for it.

"Good move calling me, Icarus," she laughs. "If you stick around, I'll teach you something." With that, she throws a can of zinc oxide at me, I catch it and we return in separate cars to the office. I read up on diaper rash when I get back.

Day becomes week, week becomes month and once a month is done, the calendar flips like a strobe light. I sit on a couch and decide to stand. An entire room moves while cockroaches defy gravity on pea green walls and stucco ceilings. They not only rule the night but laugh and party during the day. They are so at home, they give up the charade of scurry and evade. The big ones grow familiar and I might as well buy presents and bake a birthday cake for them. And the hell of it is, back in my Landing Zone, where I rule the day but not the night, there is a knock at my door at the end of the month, and

I hand over my rent check to a cockroach dressed up in a landlady suit. I fall for it every time.

Toddlers crawl over *Playboy* magazines while wary pimps watch me talk with their ladies and check for bruises, not just on the children. I learn quickly the forensics of bruising; the nice fresh dark and purple ones with the swelling. The more mature yellow ones fade to just a hint of green. A cigarette burn is crusty on the top, perfectly round and rather fascinating to see on the back of a six-year-old boy. A man gestures with a baseball bat. We already snatch three of his babies and are about to cradle rob this one.

"You bastards!" he says, tapping the bat on his palm. "I am going where you can't find me and have a hundred babies."

"Your master's gone away," I tell him while the cops efficiently immobilize his sorry arse.

Like an idiot, just before my furlough at the six-month mark, I hear myself volunteer to help out on calls. Lon Chaney always joins me when I volunteer. He helps me debrief.

"Jeezis! Lon," I tell him over smashes of rye in my dog-hole, "it is Friday night just before five. The atomic clock cooks off the intensity of the week and I suck tobacco smoke into my lungs so deep, my toes tingle. I trip the light fantastic into a weekend of no plans and who cares? People leave already, make wise cracks and I dodge a wadded ball of paper."

"Sucks to be you, Jimmy!" someone says.

They know I walk out the second-hand tick to the exact stroke of five. The night Marines come on duty then and I stop walking point.

Paula is one of the good ones. I see her scribble furiously. The phone presses into the side of her head. Five o'clock comes and goes, I am off duty and the supervisors are gone. Paula sets down her pen, rubs the back of her neck and nods her head in the ritual of a phone call soon to be complete. She hangs up, I stub my cigarette and walk over.

"One of my families is in trouble," she says as if in a trance. "Neighbours hear her yelling and call it in. We removed her older daughter last year. Sally has a temper that won't be fixed. There goes my Friday night."

"Mine too," I tell her.

Paula calls it into the police. An unmarked cruiser is already there when we turn onto the street. A shimmer of light cools the leaves of ash trees along the urban boulevard and a breeze paints everything in a flutter of motion. The dapple would be pretty if we had time to listen to it. Old men in undershirts sip beer on their porches and watch the work day end. Their relief fills me with envy.

We pass the cruiser and I nod to the two officers who notice us well before our approach. I see their second sense click-in, along with that look-you-up-and-down-thing they perfect.

"Shit, Paula. Why do cops make me want to confess things I do not do?" I laugh to break the tension.

It is the tired time, at the cusp. Where hard work will sigh into dinner soon and nobody really looks at us. I exit the Chevelle and walk back to make contact and brief the cops. Paula opens her black book and consults her notes. She exits the car and I walk behind her and up onto a porch. Paula has been here before. The door on the left opens to an angle of wooden stairs that ascend to a small landing and closed door. Even from the bottom of the stairs I see the varnish crack in a million places. Paula does not talk now. She has that serious look in her eyes. The same one I get when I focus. It is like the dull stare of a shark. Her client is young and she tries to do her best. I hear she shook-the-shit out of her first child and turns her into a rag doll. She did not mean to, nobody does. The second toddler is watched over by Cherubim and Court Order, once every two weeks for scheduled visits and whenever the hell we feel like it, at irregular intervals. What we call "unscheduled visits" in our case notes. Baby snatchers and cradle robbers with a little orange card with our signature on the back.

It is no surprise when Paula taps on the door and calls out: "Sally, it's Paula. Come and open the door, hon.'"

Sally opens the door and looks surprised to see me with Paula. She shows some involuntary femininity and steps back to usher us in. She goes to the kitchen table to fetch her smokes and light up. She talks friendly and casual and unsurprised. The ease makes me suspicious. Paula too. She turns on the charm and the effect is like magic. Sally is less skittery and less contrived.

"You are probably here to see Stinky," she says. "I just put him down." She aims her head to the left where a bedroom door is ajar.

I hear little squeak noises come from the room: innocent toddler sing-babble. I can tell he is in a crib.

It is hot and stuffy. No money for an air conditioner. A fan holds a sash open, not able to oscillate but gratefully pumping bona fide air into an otherwise sweaty room. The white walls look damp. The clutter in the sink suggests the routine is off. If I could interview the room, this one says it is so freaking depressed, there is nothing to eat and I hate it here, let me out. I am in spirit form and sense that something is clearly off.

Paula suddenly cuts to the quick. She has that relationship with her. I can tell the mom sees it coming. Still she winces at Paula's tone.

"We got a call from the community, hon."

"Who?"

"Is not the point," Paula deflects with some tone. The mother backs down, takes a drag from her cigarette, sits and vies for control.

I take this as a cue. Like a prick I get up, open the fridge, look inside and unbalance the hell out of her. It is very intrusive and I don't know where I learn it.

"Seems a little empty," I say. "Why don't I let the two of you talk. Mind if I check on your little guy?"

Sally lights another smoke and seems to relax when I leave to go to the bedroom.

"Hey, Little Guy," I coo gently as I open the door and smile. The sun throws shadows around the room now and I feel dull and tired.

Stinky is in diapers. He grins and hauls himself up by the rails, wobbles a bit and then rests his arms. He is a pro at it and it is cute to watch. He is easy to engage. I touch his little fingers, make baby sounds and in the available light, I look over his torso, down his chubby legs, up his other side, to his arms. I inspect both and shift my gaze to his cheeks and forehead. I rub his tiny blonde hair at the crown to check for lumps. Like an X-ray I inspect his ribs. I see no apparent soft tissue bruises. I see no blotches on rib bone, no lacerations or abrasions. There are no left-over yellow tinges on his cheeks that I might miss the first time. He looks clean and happy. His diaper is dry. No tell-tale signs of rash.

"Hey, Little Man," I sing and he grins. "Are you okay? Anything happen, hon? Can you tell me?"

The caller complains to Paula that she hears yelling and scream-ing and the baby is a little prick. The caller says she saw Sally drunk yesterday and with some guy.

I hear Paula grow more direct. She tells the mom the allegations. "I didn't hit him," she says. "Yes, I had a drink and the guy is an asshole, Paula. I always find assholes. I don't fucking know why."

Time passes. She has another smoke. The light starts to change windows. I am sure the cops wonder what goes on. Paula and I lose ground. The mom admits to some of the information, the toddler is clean; yet still we both feel something is not right. By now I trust my intuition in the Charred City.

Paula tells me on the way over, the older daughter got shaken baby syndrome. She will never be normal now. Vegetable is the shitty word we use and it spooks me.

The fear of responsibility will do that. I do not want to get this wrong. It is not like pounding S-irons into soft ties all morning at the creosote plant. It is frightening to do your best and come up short. Hard to live with. Like a siren call, the week's burn-out tempts me to pack it in; surely our drop-in is deterrent enough. We won't get much more out of her and besides, Paula is scheduled to come back Tuesday. I die to go home, shower and go out. C'mon, it is Friday and I am young.

Paula is frustrated but it barely shows. She runs out of approach-es. I know the feeling. I can only approach a thing from so many angles and then an interview locks itself into a stalemate. I have no idea where I learn this but it is true.

"I know something is wrong, Lon Chaney, I just know it," I say exasperated.

I decide to go back one last time and have a look at Stinky.

"Hey, Little Guy," I say again, all *sing-songy* and scared.

Stinky looks up and grins. He starts that slow bounce that tod-dlers do. He is stimulated and bounces more. He gets more spring on the mattress and I worry he will fall and smack his head. I approach him to gently steady him by the shoulders. My fingertips cup both sides of the back of his shoulders and my thumbs are gently on his scapula. I have small hands and am so tender with him. I still don't know how I learn to do that.

The light in the room is magnificent now. The last hurrah before it slips behind rooftops to say goodnight. It is then I notice my fingertips line up perfectly with the eight discolorations on little Stinky's shoulders. My thumbs match marks on his scapula. They are old and faded but familiar, like the home position on a keyboard. With a start, my sight grows keen.

"What's this, sweetheart?" I whisper and turn the babe gently into the full blaze of sun. "What a good little boy you are."

"Geezis Christ, she shook him!" I realize in awe. I try my fingertips again and my thumbs line up over the marks, perfectly.

"She's done," I hiss to myself. I actually feel elated. The fright completely leaves me. Adrenaline replaces it.

I call Paula into the room. We work efficiently after that. The mom weeps. I excuse myself. I go down the stairs and out to the street to update the police. I tell them we will snatch the baby, to remain on standby and that the mom cooperates.

I return to Paula. She and the mother pack a diaper bag, together. Paula lets her know the police will want to chat with her. She will take her son to a foster home. The mom has been through it before. She seems resigned. She lets us remove her toddler, just like that. It is an easy scoop. Guilt will do that. I see it open up her conscience to the point where she knows her truth. She knows she cannot keep her child safe. She knows she can hurt it. She knows it is wrong. I feel her relief at being rescued. It breaks my heart and I never get over how we just take her kid. I can only imagine how Stinky feels.

The cops see us on the porch and efficiently go up to talk to the mother. We agree to talk on Monday. Paula straps the toddler in. I sit in the back and talk baby-talk to it and stroke its head on the way to the emergency bed. The foster mom is a pro, we stay for a quick coffee, do the handoff, write up our notes in the car and Paula takes me back to the office.

"Nice tag-team," Paula says in the parking lot. "Thank you!"

"See you Monday," I say. Numb now and too tired to have fun.

I have another smash with Lon Chaney and then crawl off to bed, careful to check for roaches before I turn out the light.

During the night there are no dreams. I come to, in spirit form, free from gravity and time and space. I am a nighthawk in *Oncewuz*, capable of nocturnal sight and flight at sharp angles through vernal cones of light, ponding around the asphalt.

Night vision truly has a weird green effect but it illuminates a different reality.

I see a man's entire face grimace like a bat in repose. They call it burn-out. It is not pretty to witness. He still has his lungs, still believes in the truth of old nobilities but his heart is fungal and oily and wretched, really. When the phone rings, his cringe is matter-of-fact, a built-in part of him. The effect on me is like the shudder before a punch to the head. His voice turns brittle then and there is an odour like burning hair. I see acid drip off his heart and lungs, watch it trickle from on high to its lowest state of rest so that everything he says has the property of a leak in the basement. Where it appears is not the source of how it began. I like him but I cannot stay near him. It is sad really, because in a way I see he tries to help us learn to keep perspective. His misery is an unintended gift to our reality. He speaks through flames that immolate his heart but do not cook it off into charcoal. I sense it will take another year to do that. He is a lifer and has put in more years than all the innocence in the days before apps, when boys walk the earth. I bring him a coffee once in a while, when I am back from a search and destroy mission in the Charred City. I sign off the mileage on a clipboard in the Chevelle and buy two small coffees, no butch. I am careful not to accept his invitation to go around for a beer after work. He is one of Us and I am one of Him. If I get closer, I know I will taste acid, too. There are one or two others, who pat him, but I see that most avoid. The ones that do go to lunch with him are "B-teaming" and not that good at what we do. The ratio and proportion of toxicity glows truly in the nocturnal green light between buddies.

By sheer will, I lift off to get loft. The air is moist and heavy and the tail lights of cars turn the entire block into a fluid Monet. I hover over the faint glow of the laundromat, correct course and glide south into the bowels of the Charred City. The Landing Zone is behind me. As an afterthought to comfort, I peer under my arm to make out the oval blink of the donut shop and I lust after a honey cruller. They are so warm when they come out of the oven.

There is a carnival of blues and greens, reds and whites. The shape of a tree looks majestic from on high. Each one is a grand arboreal form with an anatomy of usefulness that cannot be seen from the ground. My gaze is acute in an atmosphere smeared with colour. The lumen reflects the moisture of countless pairs of raccoon eyes that gaze upwards from the branches. They snuggle in to bear witness to the comings and goings of spirits.

I am past the box stores and high-rises and over the Big Street now. The ground streaks expectantly below, stop-and-go-to-slow like a meteorite shower. West and well below the river in the north, I alight in the kill zone. My mind works overtime and the effect is like an X-ray. I see things not visible in the daylight. All doors are open, there are no walls to conceal, no porches to come outside and speak from. Activity knots into a cluster and the cluster transforms into a sense of teaming. The teaming gives way to a deeper effect of colony and the colony parts around me when I walk straight into it. Thought and affection exhale and form landscapes so fluid they open senses I am surprised I possess. I smell urinous bogs, watch sand dunes form and disintegrate into rocky crags I can touch and enter. Shadows on the wall dance and I descend with them into caverns filled with B-movie lizards, stupid floppy dorsal sails and menacing tongues.

"*Buh dee chee chee!*" I cry out for effect and it echoes back tenfold.

Polaroid photos litter the cavern floor like guano. There are so many the gloss renders an effect like the moisture of newly fallen tears. Two men in cowboy hats get their *doinks* sucked by boys and girls and teenagers. Some are under obvious duress. Some actually look blissful. I see their exaggerated glee is masked by the glaze of narcotics. There is a wall at the back of the cavern. I see man after man, down on his haunches. They flick the photos: thumb, two fingers and wrist snap, intent to see who gets the card closest; to see who will win the lot and take it all home to the privacy of his own mind.

One by one, I drag their sorry arses to court. We all take turns. They show up in suits or what passes as good clothes or fuck it, they show up and some of them cry and some of them look pissed off to be caught. Most of them get two years less a day. I get a day or two out of the Charred City, time to catch up on my paperwork and behold the fruit of my labour in a farm land of decay.

And what is it with the too much spit in the mouth? In another part of the colonies couple after couple disintegrate and take their children with them. Bruise after bruise, cigarette after cigarette, round crusty burn after round crusty burn. I learn the telephone numbers for the roach and lice marines by heart. No age or stage untouched. Babies are born, that holy tableaux, and I use my little orange card to keep the infants on heavenly wards while mothers discharge home with screams to tear my eyes out. Later when I go to visit them, some actually thank me. Slowly, not on my watch, my colleagues help them reunite; they support their strength and when it is safe, discharge them back into life.

Over by a knoll, I meet the most wonderful people; kind, generous; as authentic as the day is long. There are so many of them. They teach me patience, acceptance and a genuine-ness of being that expands my mind. They open corridors of heart I do not think I possess. I check my judgement at the door like a pair of snowboots, not wanting to sully their humanity. They bind my wounds and take me to an Inn I never intend on going to.

"I am fluent with zinc oxide now," I confess proudly to Lon Chaney over a smash of rye on the weekend. "And I make friends with cops and nurses, too."

And that is the hell and strange draw of the Charred City. Lesson upon lesson offered relentlessly at its most desperate hour by souls who are not the sum total of problem but who carry and stoke an ambergris of humanity that is eternal.

"Jimmy Crack Corn and I don't care," Lon mocks me.

"You are an asshole, Lon Chaney," I tell him straight to his face. "Why don't you go out to the EverGreens and howl at the moon? You know, rip your clothes and do that transformation thing you do before you turn into a shit-head."

"Don't go horror movie on me, Jimmy. Seems like you change, not me. Don't kid yourself, Arse-face."

"Who dies and makes you so freaking mean," I tell him and walk out of the bar in a huff.

I suppose the coons in the trees see me come back but I have no recollection of my return. There is a donut left in the bag and an empty coffee container in the sink when I get up to go to work. Last night I saw the exact moment when innocence leaves. Why me, for Christ's sake? Why do I get to see that? And where does it go, anyway? I realize I don't know where I end and a young mother begins, when she places her baby safely in the bull reeds of adoption.

At work, I strap into the chair, light up a cigarette, yack a little, dodge a scrunched-up napkin and the phone rings. Repeat to infinity. The call is a follow-up to a particularly nasty snatch. The cops are in first and invite me to a briefing on their findings. We still have two souls at home under order so we run our investigation and assessment meters on full bore to discern if they are safe. When I drive by the house, it looks like a nice house from the road. There is a privet hedge and the wooden shingles are a nice touch. It is an odd thing to know door after door what goes on behind closed doors; to know the room layouts and the smell of the place. By now, we just see the headlines. Not a single citizen who thinks they know, knows a thing about the alchemy of method in the urban wars. I, Jimmy the Bleeder, just begin to get the hang of it after a long year. I cry my eyes out on furlough, the first three days at the six-month mark, and then suck it up, buttercup, past my anniversary date. Who needs to know? A couple of us hum Wagner's *Ride of the Valkyries* when we go out on calls now. It is very funny.

At the briefing a homicide cop I know hands Lon and I a legal-size red book, bound in black rings. This one is an inch thick. I read the introduction and flip through the contents. I stop at a dead child on a couch. He looks so peaceful, like he watches cartoons. He is taken from every angle and close in on the contusions. There are dimensional room layouts and a description of the sequence of events along with a million other things in cop-speak that I only guess at. It is way out of Lon's and my league where the big demons play in the Charred City. At the end of the conference, when I walk up to the homicide detective to return his book of the dead, he offers to let me hang on to it, for our own investigation and so long as I return it next Wednesday under penalty of death. When Lon and I sign in the Chevelle and walk into the office, there is a cluster of souls around my cubicle. Homicide 101 in a nutshell. The currency of respect soars through my roof, and of course the Team gives me the gears on it.

"Jimmy, you Bleeder! Why did they give that to you of all Apes?" is the prevailing commentary.

"Because I am amazing and god's gift to cradle robbing," I tell them simply. The group disperses when two supervisors swing by to inspect my treasure. The generous gift of death-knowledge helps us to determine the course of our actions. After twenty-one days, the case drops off the face of my earth and I move onto the next fire.

"And the other repeat to infinity," Lon says to me on Friday night.

"It is actually not a bad week," I tell him.

Monday and Tuesday I am at the Sexual Abuse training, Part One. It is two glorious days out of the bush. Two glorious days away from phones, two good lunches and certification for stuff I already did and know. Training is always so out of synch that way. When I need it, I am inducted into the School of Hard Knocks. When I graduate from the School of Hard Knocks, my training clicks in and I get certified, legitimized and slightly more protected from lawsuits. There is a very good steak joint on the Big Street but Paula takes me for roti and soursop at the subway stop. She makes fun of the way I try to pronounce goat. On Wednesday I am with the cops, cover phones on Thursday and on Friday I turn into a Wasp. A student on placement is paired with me. The caller says a baby is "stolen" from the mother. The poor "thing" is probably over at the ex's because that "son of a bitch" is pissed off again. He "drinks like a fucking fish" and is supposed to have "zero" visitation, right now till "he sobers the fuck up!" I sign out the Chevelle, mark the mileage and show the student how to strap the baby seat in. She is young and green and frightened but, unlike me, has done a tour, babysitting her next-door neighbour's kids. I admire that. I ask her if she knows what zinc oxide does and teach her my story of how the Homemaker saves my bacon.

It is a fairly routine scoop. We are in and I am at the table like it is poker night. She stands by the door. I offer a smoke, decline a beer at 11 a.m and use my white male privilege to commiserate with the boys. For a while all we do is talk baseball. When I have control of the room and they know it, when all their macho thing is restored, it actually strikes them as noble, to give the kid back. They let me and the student walk out with an understanding of their side of the story along with messages of good will to his "bitch."

I promise to come back and visit next Friday morning. The student straps the infant in, nice and snug and talks fluent baby-speak to her in the back. Our learning is in the debrief. My latent Wasp powers emerge and we talk about joining, of unbalancing a space, of moving in so close there is no distance to get too mad. Surrounding them from the inside, I call it. When it is okay to smoke. When it is not.

"And don't make a move until you know you have control of the room," I tell her to punctuate the thing I do for months but just learn to articulate. "Get control of your fright, swallow hard, use your power and sometimes you have to make it up as you go along. Sometimes you have to "go live," I tell her.

She laughs. From time to time, when I see her with her Wasp in the office, she tells me she "went live" today and that makes me laugh.

And the morning is the weekend of the millionth day.

Toward the end of my tour, I am called out on point into the centre of the Charred City. Of course, there is no parking on the street, so I circle the block and like to inspect the variety stores for character while I wait. The shops are faceless, androgynous and bleak. Not a single one has a bike stand to crack a popsicle and this is the sole reason why stores of convenience perish as congregation points for kids.

I do find a spot long enough to parallel park the Chevelle and I tuck it in nicely just down from a donut shop. There is time for a cruller and small coffee, no butch, so I grab one and return to the car. I sip it slowly and work out a nervous jazz beat on the steering wheel with two fingers and a thumb. I await the police on a joint investigation, part of our new protocol together on the tough cases. I have a good view through the windshield of the house up the street. I wonder where the hell the police intend to park once they get here. They materialize, the way they do, suddenly, as if entering reality through a portal. And when they come, they come however they want. I love when they come slowly. It reminds me of a hammerhead shark carefree in the shallows, in no rush to decide whom to bite or when. They all have horseshoes up their arse too. Inevitably, a citizen scuppers out into the current, just as they arrive and in no time, they pull in and square away.

"I have got to learn to troll like that," I tell Lon Chaney, impressed.

"It helps if you have the white stripes, bristling antennae and strobe light waiting to be turned on, Hammerhead," he reminds me.

"Good point," I counter. I don't feel very witty. It is the time in an investigation before the adrenalin kicks in. My limbs feel heavy: My mind dull and stupid. I make note of the time in my black book, hear the car door slam and before I know it, I am at the passenger side of the cruiser. They see me approach a mile away. The senior constable grins, offers his hand and says something funny to break the tension. His partner is young and focussed. Like Fizzy and his police parade, I get this vague sense that my past has caught up to me and I have the right to remain silent. I shake his hand as well. I can see they size me up, measure my being, release it and tell it, you are free to go. We compare notes.

The call comes in from a relative. She worries about her sister and her little niece. It could be a mother calling, a neighbour, a citizen, a pissed-off ex, a colleague, another pissed-off ex, anybody, frankly, who cannot live and should not live with that little voice inside that says something is wrong, I know it and I have to do something about it. In the urban wars, these are the plaintive calls of a warrior. Cherubim-speech to men and women. Our chance to right a wrong.

"Turns out the dad is at work," I tell them. "The mom knows we are here and who made the call. The little girl is home."

For some reason, the cops let me walk point. I knock on the door. The mother opens it and lets us in. The little girl is at the coffee table and watches television. There is an empty glass of milk on the table. I know a lot about her already. She is a big girl, almost four and will start playschool soon. She is quiet and does not talk much. She has a cat named Peach. The cops know a little bit about the dad because he is known to them for yelling at his wife, last year. The mother is frightened. There is worry around her eyes. Still, there is something resolute about her. We all sense it. The irony of three men investigating passes through me and then leaves. The thing is in the room. The entity not-visible. The unspoken thing whose shape will instantly appear the minute it is named. It is like those clever camouflage pictures of nature. Can you find the snake in this picture?

Can you spot the elephant in this mist? Do you know this man is an asshole?

Somebody told me, somebody who really knew, the key to the ability to see the animal in the picture is to think dirty. Think the worst first, and work it back out from there. It is the exact opposite of the benefit of the doubt. The skilled soul will factor that benefit in too, or let it sit like leaven and see what happens depending on the angle. But a lot happens in an interview and we don't have forever to speculate. Thinking dirty protects me from what I hear. It is an odd effect. Horror is then rendered conversational. I am not sure where I learn that.

I approach the little coffee table and sit down on the rug opposite the girl. I tell her my name. I ask her if it is okay if I sit with her and if she likes to draw. Peach comes over to sniff me and rub her eye and whiskers against my knee. The little girl tells me that Peach likes me. I tell her that I like Peach. She tells me what treats Peach likes to eat and she, herself likes those chocolate lady fingers for her treat. Her dad likes to give them to her. I have not asked her about her dad. I ask her if she likes sponge toffee and tell her that anytime someone puts chocolate on sponge toffee, I am so happy. I can't remember the name of the chocolate bar though and she tells me its name. She looks triumphant. I thank her and she giggles. In time, she is ready to draw. I have crayons and that nice manila-style colouring paper and it feels a bit like school. The first couple of drawings are for her. The next drawing is for me. We have a little chat about why I am here, why my police friends are here and without being told or scripted, I lead her to understand that she can draw out what happens with Daddy. She nods and I know it is time to name the elephant and bring him into the room so we can see what we are all up against. It is the saddest thing to be there at the exact moment the elephant comes into a little person's life. There is so much innocence stolen but the innocence that is left is beyond Holy and guarded by Cherubim, in full view. The light is Celestial then, brighter than white and there is not one thing that matters more.

On the left is a stick drawing of Daddy. Peach is in the right corner eating treats out of her bowl. Mommy is not in the picture. She is shopping. Daddy has lady fingers in his hand. There are more lady fingers than actual fingers and she uses a nice brown for them. She uses orange for Daddy's big *pee-pee thing*. She puts some brown on it too. She tells me that is where *pee pee* comes out. She asks if I have a white crayon and I take it out of the box and tenderly hand it to her. One of the cops comes over to watch. The older one talks quietly with the mother. The little girl draws what looks like tears coming out of Daddy's doink. "Tell me about that," I ask her.

"This is Daddy's sticky stuff," she says as a matter of fact.

The mom starts to cry and she so needs to get it off her chest. It is hard to be completely accurate. The cops and I make the elephant out to be a year old or somewhere close to that.

It is five to five and the second hand is the only hand worth watching. I have my party. A blue paper napkin with cake still on it, bounces off my forehead and falls into my ashtray. There is laughter. Everyone leaves. Why I am on phones on the eleventh minute of the eleventh hour of my eleventh day comes down to the hand I am dealt. My partner is on holidays. We are short-staffed. Even though my brain is mush and our policy strongly suggests that short-timers have a tendency to be useless the last week, I am asked with a grin if I would not mind sucking it up. What is one more shift after two years, two months, two days and an honourable discharge, replete with urban combat medal and a purple heart? At three minutes to five, I suck smoke so deep into my lungs I think of Clarence the Drug-Addled Lion in the laneways of *Oncewuz*. I cannot believe when the phone rings. It has to be the record. Two minutes to five. In 120 seconds, night duty clicks in. My phone won't ring, but until then, we rule the day. It works the other way around when the sun comes up so the system is fair. It takes a special breed of cat to be a night fighter. At least during the daylight, I see what I am up against. People are different at night. Elephants tend to get pissed off when called out of the dark.

In any case there is a woman on the phone. The timbral on her voice sounds vaguely familiar but muscle memory clicks in. Pen replaces cigarette, case-form pushes away ashtray. The woman cries. It is Friday and she cannot cope. *Gawddammit*, she needs a break from her kids, just for the weekend, and if I don't come out immediately, she can't tell me what she will do. I stand and look over my cubicle for backup. We might need an emergency bed for two children, one of them still in diapers. Most of the office is cleared out. It is just Paula and she is on the phone too.

I do my best to listen and calm, calm and support. Together, we pursue resources. "Are there any relatives that can take the children and give you the break you need?"

"No, I am alone," she says.

It goes like this for a while and there is a certain tipping point, almost like a scale, and each coin is a degree of risk. There are at least five coins now in the go-out-and-investigate side. The balance tips and I thank the women for reaching out and asking for support. I let her know that I will be there inside of thirty minutes and that together we will work out a good plan.

This is when she tells me to please bring out a case of zinc oxide when I come and she will serve me *goooat* and soursop.

"It is not a bad way to be drummed out," I tell Lon Chaney, that night over shots of rye in an Inn, near the laundromat.

"Werewolf!" he cries.

That night, I am not in spirit form. I actually have a nightmare. I dream I am chased by an angry mob with torches through the streets of the Charred City. My shirt is ripped from beating my breast and my pants are cinched at the waist with a rope. There is weeping and gnashing of teeth. I am out of breath—in need of sanctuary. The moon is out in full and I glance at it in desperation. The light falls right across my eyes. I practically taste melodrama and it is thick, like syrup. I am seized by the crowd. Somebody jams a torch into my face and I can see him grimace and go: "See? See?" They all look like bats. There is the low rumble of a Triumph motorcycle. A Greaseball guns it for me. I rip free from the mob, mount the bike and feel the wind on my face in full throttle. I look over my shoulder in time to see the complete immolation of Lon Chaney. He smiles at me through the flames.

North now of the Charred City, I stop at a variety store for a pack of smokes. I fight the urge to look in the garbage drum. When I emerge, the motorcycle is gone and there is Old Gray and the milk wagon. What a scoundrel! The second I appear, he dumps his load of road apples onto the parking lot. He turns his head in that droll, lopsided way to look at me with both eyes. Suddenly I feel old and like my father. It is not unpleasant but for a time it is just me and Gray and I am alone. I think of Dug Hill and I think of cornerstones. My mind goes off into the stratosphere to find peace.

The sixth dinosaur, the one I cannot remember, turns out to be a brontosaurus. She is a girl-dinosaur with a beautiful long neck in proportion to the length of her tail. Her name is Maria. She has four sturdy legs, well spaced and is very difficult to tip over. Her colour is a blend of purple and indigo and it is quite becoming. The Stegosaurus is sweet on her but frankly, with all those spikes and plates along his back, he is difficult to hug and harder to kiss. Orange is not her colour. It is the green tyrannosaurus rex that catches her eye. He is about the same height as her, which means he can make eye contact, and if he can make eye contact they can see into one another's spirits and talk. She thinks that is important in a Jurassic relationship. So does he. For a while, the tyrannosaurus rex (whose colour is a beautiful green blended with some indigo, like her) does not really notice the brontosaurus. He has that angry young dinosaur thing going on, his type all do, and maybe it is because he has those useless forearms with the dorky claws on the end. Still, he cuts a fine figure. His haunches are rather sexy and he too stands erect with sturdy legs. He is difficult but not impossible to tip over.

What she likes about him is that he has the type of eyes that constantly peer into the distance. They are so resolute. It is not like he searches. It is quite the opposite. What she loves is that he stands on two legs and takes a metaview. "He is not searching," she says to herself, while brushing her thick skin. "He is striding out into his dreams. Besides, he is kind and plays nicely with the other dinosaurs. There is an innocence about him that is slightly out of view. I like that in a dinosaur." Sometimes she thinks he should take a pill though, and lighten up and what is it with the roar-thing all of the time?

One day, the six dinosaurs are in a circle, dancing. Even the dorky B-Team dinosaur with the sail on his back dances. Most of us think he looks more like a reptile than a dinosaur. Because he looks like he just walks off the set of *Journey to the Centre of the Earth*, we make him into a boy or a girl, depending on what game we play.

He is versatile as a scapegoat but what saves him is his colour. To be honest, all of us love that shade of yellow and the orange mix in his or her sail is quite attractive. The six dinosaurs are happy today. Eric Dolphy plays his flute like a bird, his alto like a hyena and his bass clarinet like a honking raptor. Do-si-do and promenade your partner. The sun streams through the window. A million dust mites float like tiny sugar plum fairies or volcanic ash over this blissful play scape. The effect is romantic. The other four dinosaurs do not see it coming. My God, the tyrannosaurus rex and the brontosaurus are engaged! He loves the way she laughs. It is a full-body laugh and it tempers his growl so that he laughs too. The two of them toddle off to the right behind a pillow. When they return, they are married! I tenderly pick up the remaining four dinosaurs and put them in their little linen bag. They are precious to me, iconic some might say. Soon, in the spring, when the trilliums and trout lilies and bloodroot first say hello from the soil and the Jack-in-the-pulpits testify in clusters from the forest floor, two baby dinosaurs are born. The Daddy dinosaur and the mommy dinosaur are so happy. They dance the light fantastic on their tails. It is funny to watch. Hands bring them together and they kiss and kiss and kiss. There is no extra spit in their mouths because they are made of soft plastic. The baby dinosaurs love to play. Daddy Dinosaur takes them to the land of *Oncewuz* to play in the Bay of Tranquility. (When they are older, he will take them to the River of Joy to swing off the rope.) The daddy dinosaur will never take them up to the Purdy for he is a suck now, and does not want his baby dinosaurs to get killed. "Do as I say and not as I do," he tells his baby dinosaurs and realizes he is an arse for saying it.

"And the other Jimmy Crack Corn," his babies tell him.

"*Buh dee chee chee,*" I say.

A screen door whines and then bangs three times. There is giggling. The grass feels soft on the soles of my feet. There are pine trees everywhere. Red pines, white pines and a majestic blue spruce that stands tall and looks like the laird of the land. I sidestep the brown dry needles, careful not to prick a toe. The sky is big and blue and wide and blue. I breathe deeply and hold it to feel my chest expand. A loon flies low to kiss the water with her wings and then finds loft to disappear into a bright cozy ball of sun. I cross a ribbon of asphalt, my two lambs in tow. It bakes our feet and we scuttle across to bathe them in the cool sand at the edge of the lake. Two blue bottle dragonflies stop what they do, hover, laugh and then dart off between the blades of spikey water grass. We are quiet as a gazelle then, careful not to thunder up to the lily pads and pickerel weed. One leopard frog is alert. He does see us, leaps and plops off into the water. It is beautiful to see him dart through the weeds and hide. I imagine he tastes like chicken. Some arse across the lake washes their hair and the telltale sign of phosphate suds clings to our stand of bull reeds. They do their best to filter the lake and keep it clean. Our gaze is scientific. We scan the edge of the waterscape with practised eyes. I am pleased that our children know how to do that. Half knot of wood, half blob of muck, I point to the bulbous eyes of a bull frog. He looks so cozy in his slime. There are shushes and careful steps, one at a painful time, toes first, into the water. The mud is squishy, the odour, primordial. I bend over, cup my hands and lift the amphibian into the cumbersome world of gravity. His legs look exactly like frogs' legs, bent inward at the knee. They dangle so long and low and we dub him *Frogzilla*. My daughter touches his mouth with the tip of her finger.

We all take turns holding him and then my son carefully replaces him in his gumbo of muck and lily. A water snake glides in ribbons towards a dock and disappears under it without even ducking her head. Silly water bugs zig-zag out of the way. The movement is so dorky we have to try it ourselves.

The dock is dry and gray, warm and beautiful. Water laps under the frame and taps out a sucking beat. We are on our chests now, to look at the graceful daddy longlegs. There are other spiders too and they scare me. Mosquitoes and tiny dusk bugs litter their webs.

My son unhitches the rope to our large inflatable dinghy. His sister already sits at the bow. She displaces so little water, she looks like a monarch butterfly sailing proudly through the breeze on a stick. I climb in and of course, there are giggles as the bow rises to the sky. I paddle us out, away from the dock to a spot a little deeper. We barely see the icky tops of weeds down below.

This morning I am asked to play "Titanic." Believe me, I don't have to be begged to do it. When it is time, we get the story line going. In the days before apps, when boys and girls walk the earth, let there be melodrama.

"Daddy, watch out! There is an iceberg coming!"

"Splash it away!" I say.

The children drive it back and we are safe.

"What ever you do, you must not fall asleep on watch," I order.

Soon there is snoring.

"Oh no!" I cry. "What have we done? Iceberg! Iceberg off the starboard side!"

I shift to my knees and lean back to make the bow point to the sky. The children scupper topside.

"Hang on for dear life, maties," I yell at the top of my lungs. "We take on water!"

The children scream the beautiful screech of the schoolyard. It is like birdsong.

"We are sinking! No, no, it cannot be. We are doomed!" I cry and shift to stand fully erect at the stern. I salute the sky.

It is so cute to see the children splayed for dear life on the rubber bow. They know what is coming. Daddy's balance is not that good. My daughter cannot hang on and I see her disappear over the top. I hear her plop into the water. The cackle of my son's delight is wet to my ears. There is an explosion, the dinghy rockets into the sky and falls smack on top of the three of us. I look below to see my son, on top of my daughter as they frantically kick and squirm like little frogs. I reach down and gently grab my daughter under an arm to guide her sputtering to the surface. It is the moment of hesitation, whether to laugh or cry for O the trauma! Our three faces are inches from one another as we tread water. Our noses touch, our foreheads gently bonk and their buoyancy under my arms is like a life preserver.

I am on the buckboard of Old Gray now. The blue tail flies are out and I swish them away with the hickory broom. Gray shudders and soon, his clip clops take us east and to the north, over the River and into the highlands. Perhaps there is a reality more exquisite than this one. An atmosphere that animates and informs the earth of my mind. I am drawn to that affection and soon, I am aware of cattle trails, again. They riddle the terrain underneath Old Gray's hooves.

Little worn troughs like arteries trace and wander, bunch up and depart in every direction I imagine. I am far into my choice to get good at something I did not set out to do. It is my exclusive trail, a providence clearly not of my own design. Strangely, the more I travel along it, the more freedom I possess and the possession becomes a currency of power. My choices mature and take on a depth of intentional meaning. I am less random. Old Gray senses it. There is a graceful pride in his gait now. He fairly prances as if on parade. His noble mane flows with each nod and bob.

"What do you want to be a Do-gooder for," I tease him.

I sense a funky odour and look over my shoulder at the apples that litter the ground below.

My trail becomes a path and the path widens to become a lane. We travel through an apple grove and I smell the sweet fermentation. Cicadas begin their high pitch. The tall grass is warm and yields to bodysurf a breeze. A yellow-tail hawk defines his territory from on high. I blink when she flies through the sun. The grasslands give way to olive groves. The trees dance in gyres up the gentle rolls of the foothills. Old Gray carries on to take me higher and steeper into the pines. The air is cool and I begin to see my breath. It is rock now, boulder and crag. The top of the mountain is defined by a small clearing, which opens up carefully into the outcrop of a wide cliff. It is here that Old Gray comes to a halt.

He is a sweetheart and lets me place my hand under his chin to kiss his nose. Gently, I run my arm down each foreleg which he patiently lifts. I clean out the frogs of his hooves with a little pick, to tenderly prevent any irritation. I brush him, click my tongue to turn him, lead him to the path and with an affectionate pat, send him down the mountain. He is such a loyal Ape. When I turn, to behold the valley, I still smell him on my hands.

I possess a new acuity. The valley opens up before me. My sight focuses like a binocular. I worry that my nose is slim; that it grows sharper and that my inner face in repose, gets that perennially pissed-off bird-of-prey look. I slowly sweep my gaze in jerky intervals, east then west, farther north along a plane to skim the tops of pines. I tilt my head. My gaze leads me out and away and across the valley floor to the base of a second mountain. The oaks, the beeches, the maples are massive. Their florets mass together, pack tightly, burst and give the effect of a bubbling green cauldron, steaming, overflowing, higher and higher to an outcrop of granite. Even at a distance, the granite looks cold and hard and permanent. I see the suggestion of a ledge, the mouth of a cave and now I stand at its threshold to look up into the yaw. It is dark. The echo of moisture somewhere within leaves the impression of tears and an unplumbed depth of weeping that fills me with a sense of dread. I shuck off that veil and my heart fills with a desire to know, to understand and to mend. I walk forward and down. I rub my hand along the rock. Pockets of quartz appear, dusky with hints of red rust or interior smoke. Deeper I descend past precious metals I can alternately name and not-name. Time after time I stretch beyond my experience, beyond my ability, vulnerable like a flame protected by a cupped hand, held out to guide my resolute way.

In the lands of *Neverwuz*, north of the Charred City, there lies, nestled between the high rises and discarded syringes, a school. Some thought has gone into its location for it is buffered by a ring of trees. The ring of trees defines an inviting space that exudes a sense of order and maybe even a slight promise that I will get better if I come here. In the déjà vu that life offers, I find it a close replica to the Baby Park in *Oncewuz*. There is a set of swings here. A large square sandbox with triangles in the corner to sit on: plenty of open grass to play catch. The requisite patch of asphalt provides enough room to shoot hoops. There is a front entrance, a side door and room between the trees and the brick walls to run in opposite directions around the school. I am led here by six soft plastic dinosaurs and a growing literacy of the language of play.

The school is filled with "not in my backyard" children whose masters have all gone away and the other Jimmy Crack Corn, they don't care. Why should they?

They are rejects, retards, shit-heads, stinkies, bad boys and bad girls, cross-eyed, Dummies, fucked up and mad. Who actually wants them in their school? Bridges have been burnt. They do not get along with other kids, tend to swear at teachers or perform variations on what we call a melt-down. A melt-down is random. Sometimes they appear during transitions between activities in class or upon return from recess to the classroom. Some of these little bleeders can not even play outside without getting into it with another child. What the hell?

They break things. Some refuse to do work, or tear it up when they complete it.

The odd one will miss the toilet and finger-paint. The parents will be the first to tell you that suspension does not work, and later, when they get to know you, which is to say, trust you, they might ask for help and tell you they are exhausted. They might not ever trust you. What I love about the parents is that to a soul, they love their children and that love is like giving a bear hug to a porcupine. I am not sure how they do it, but there is a threshold in our humanity that will not be breached. Survival renders love to its most elemental form and there is a beauty to that that is as powerful as it is rare. Only a DoGooder will tell you that. I receive a flashback and the only good part of it is that Fizzy is back in the picture!

"Fizzy, I miss you, you crazy arse!"

"*Buh dee chee chee*," he says.

Fizzy and I stand on the second floor of our middle school. We work in a pair to complete a project and the teacher sends us to the library. It is a wonderful thing to be alone in the corridor of a school. Time slows to a standstill. We know every teacher behind every door and the grades in them. I hear the murmur of voices when we pass each threshold. I tell Fizzy not to peek through the window, but inevitably we have to. We take a long drink from both fountains, stop to read the bulletin board and comment on the apes whose poetry is framed in construction paper and even letters. We go down the stairs to the first floor and walk the length of that hall. We are careful not to linger near the office and drink from both fountains. We stop to take a piss. Our rounds complete, we climb the landing back to the second floor. The library is on the left. I hear a yell. A door swings open on the right and a grade seven girl is made to sit at a desk outside of her room. She breathes heavily. Her hair is blonde, short and tangled. She is new to our school and we are not sure of her name. Rosella, I think. Somebody says she smells like cat-piss but Fizzy and I will never know. We don't intend to get that close. As we approach her, she looks up. Her eyes rage but because we are the same age, I can tell she is desperate and humiliated beyond belief. I can feel her need to cry. As if to make a point, she gets up, laughs and proceeds to shove the desk down the stairs and onto the landing. A leg breaks off. The principal comes up the stairs with a gym teacher and they escort her to the office. When the three of them breeze by us, I smell her.

"She really does smell like cat-piss, Fizzy," I say

We go to the library and get a whole lot of nothing done in a short amount of time. More freaking homework for the weekend. When I return on Monday, Rosella is gone and I never see her again.

So, it is with some sense of completion that I walk up the stairs of this new school, open up the door and report to the office. I meet my colleagues, the principal, the clinical supervisor, get the tour, feel the hum of the classrooms and meet the teachers and child and youth workers. By the end of the day, I have a starting caseload of thirteen Stinky's and counting, along with their families. I open my bag and place my six soft plastic dinosaurs in a line on my desk. The Do-Gooder is in.

In the morning, after announcements, I introduce myself to a ten-year-old boy.

He is wary at first and takes sanctuary in the chair opposite me. A table is between us. On the table are six dinosaurs, some pristine Play-Doh, paper, pencils and other drawing material. The supply, like me, is limited but inviting.

He props his head on his hand and listens to the purpose of our meeting. In forty-five minutes, I will walk him back to his class. We will meet once a week over the next couple months. I want to go slow with him. There is a lot going on in his life. Even at his young age, he has already met five or six Do-Gooders at the going rate of a dime a dozen.

After some chatter, I sense he grows comfortable:

"Let's play 'Find the picture,'" I say. "Grab a pencil and close your eyes. When I say go, start to scribble over the entire sheet and when I say stop, open your eyes. When you open your eyes, there is a picture in the drawing that only you see. Pick up a crayon and colour it in to reveal what it is."

It is a simple exercise and a way to connect. Sometimes, the picture found in the scribble is random and funny and sometimes there are clues. A clue is an impression, a thing to watch for in the hum of intuition and foreknowledge. The fun part of 'Find the picture' is that he can direct the play as well; ask me to close my eyes, scribble, stop and colour in what I see. Sometimes, the picture found in my scribble is random and funny and sometimes, the boy gets clues. His clue is a feeling of safety based on too many years of wariness, worry and the fact that adults in his life have a tendency to love him, hit him or leave him. While cynicism comes with age and potency of experience, his young heart is still willing to be called by name so that his innocence may be repaired by play and other forms of consistent magic. It is sacred, really, to be witness to the first tender shoots of trust offered. It is like a new plant eager to reclaim the charred forest floor. I see bloodroots again: trout lilies and trilliums, red, variegated and white. The first Jack-in-the-pulpit is a thrill. Like a time-lapse photo, a tiny bud penetrates the sky from the hidden safety of earth. Slowly, it stretches its stem, leaves burst forth, inch by inch and begin to cup around a striped brown trumpet which now stands tall and ready to testify from its pulpit. The amazing thing is that the wildflower is already present and waits patiently for me to see it. When I do see it and I can see it, my eyes acquire the literacy of the forest floor. There are so many flowers. I no longer focus on what is burnt. I see what is not burnt and suddenly, I realize the green thrill of life bursts up both within me and outside of me. Green mist hovers along the forest floor, like moss but not moss and like finger-painting, slowly pushes back the blackness a foot of soil at a time. I have seen it.

"Hi, how are you. Did you have a good week? I see you want to draw today. Are you ready to try something new? Close your eyes and imagine with me. You are on the ledge of a tall mountain. You look across a long valley and spot a mountain in the distance. You can make out a ledge there too. There is an opening. It looks like the mouth of a cave. In a moment, you have wings and fly over and stand at the mouth of the cave. It is dark inside but somehow you can see. You go in and the cave goes down and down and at the bottom you see the door to a cavern. You approach the door, open it and enter. Open your eyes and draw what you see in your cavern."

I make my way down the corridor and my shins tell me that the ground levels off. The light cast from the match in my cupped hand reveals a door. A wind blows the flame out and I am left in darkness so thick it chokes me. I lean against the quartz and it feels wet upon my cheek. The corridor is weeping. I am weeping. My heart flushes with dread. The dread aches and feels like a weight that is too heavy to carry. I curse the gravity with a rage so deep, I feel it scratch my vocal chords, tighten the muscles around my neck and make my teeth sore. I see my fists clench. I stretch, close and open the fingers of both hands repeatedly. The effect is like a bellows, frankly. Open shut, open shut, air in, air out, blood in, blood out. A pulse returns. There is no return to the surface. Am I trained for this? Surely, I am not worthy. Exhaling, I reach for the door and open it to my cavern.

There is so much to see and understand. I don't have the full literacy on it. Along the walls of the cavern, pictures hang. Coloured pictures all done with crayon. You get so much rage out of a red crayon, so much depression into a black scribble, so much dream into a floating heart and brown is a study on its own. Pictures of a house, or a kinetic family drawing in live action, all figures placed strategically as clues. The sun is over Mommy. A black cloud over Daddy. The house is on fire and flames come off dozens of babies. White angels fly grandmothers into the heavens. She can't come back, you know. Monsters, green and growling stand beside little sisters. Nobody's feet stand on solid ground. Like ghosts they walk on air.

Bats with fangs drip black blood in drops that pool in the living room. A TV is on.

So many spears hang on the walls and knives and noose after noose in perfect loops coloured in brown dangle from bedroom ceilings. There are rivers of jizz, streams of sticky stuff, doinks as big as balloons. Mean-looking babysitters growl like green tyrannosaurus rex. A yellow dinosaur with a sail on his back uses spikes to stab. The stegosaurus takes out the brontosaurus and stomps its sorry arse. Rolls over on its back and fucking puts its plates right into Uncle Jim for fucking my sister. The mommy dinosaur with the club on her tail is drunk and not even in the game. The reason the four stick figures are on the ground is because everyone is high. These birds are locked in their room and cannot get out. One by one, the six dinosaurs approach the edge of the table. They step forward and fall with a bump into the garbage can. The next week, only three fall and I hear there are less meltdowns in class. Finally, at the end of two months, two dinosaurs dance on the tips of their tails. The next time we see one another is at recess. I teach him and a couple of his buddies how to flick baseball cards against a school wall to see who gets the closest. Another little girl uses her heel to gouge a hole in the earth. Her friend rounds it like clay on a potter's wheel. Marbles go in easier then, in the days before apps when girls walk the earth.

In my cavern is a gymnasium. There are countless mats in connected panels of four. I did not know they could be put upright on their end, splayed just so, that they support themselves like a natural-born maze. I have coloured crepe paper but we realize that toilet paper is practical for a mummy-effect. We laugh and I borrow three big rolls from the utility closet. I am invited to embalm a thirteen-year-old. We do not want to tear the toilet paper so he is patient with me. Thankfully, in the luck of the moment, it is four-ply. Gently I make a little opening for his nose and then continue higher to cover his eyes. He is completely mummified and proceeds to walk through the maze and knock some of it down. The mat makes a loud smack when it falls. It is the perfect sound. It is a punchline to a hidden narrative, punctuated by deep growls and high-pitched voices that cry for help. At the end of the maze, he stops. Like reincarnation, his arms fly up and a laughing young man steps out, his mummy completely destroyed. I welcome him to the new world and remind him that we have ten minutes left. With the remaining time, we shoot baskets with wadded tissue and keep score. We do this, six sessions in a row, I think, and each time there is increased light in the cavern. We both sense it. Suddenly, his ritual is complete. He loses interest in his "baby game" and prefers to talk while drawing.

I light a match, cup my left hand over it and proceed to pick my way up the corridor to the surface. I am conscious of the odd trance state, not just of play but of life. It is like a transistor radio at the Handy Dandy in *Oncewuz*. Some Greaseball pulls it out of his saddlebag and turns it on. We murmur our surprise that he knows where the batteries go.

"*Buh dee chee chee*," somebody says, but we grow quiet so as not to attract attention.

At first there is crackle. The Greaseball has the radio up to his ear as he tries to find a station. He finds it and we listen while Link Wray and His Wraymen do *Jack the Ripper* for two minutes and twenty-three seconds. Somebody calls him an arse and tells him to pass over the radio. Just as the song ends there is static and then the Doors do *Light My Fire*, or something. The Zippo comes out and all thumbs begin to immolate. We grow restless and go into the store to find dimes and quarters in the water of the pop cooler. Repeat to infinity.

The wattage of therapeutic play is not that much different. At first there is a rind of dissonance, a working through to find a groove, not unlike static. Then there is clarity of theme, the volume goes up or down and a full entrance into the trance of playscape is made. This should not be sustained for too long. In time, with prompts and a satisfaction that emerges from chords of understanding, the trance is gently broken. There is static and then the new channel to reality. When it works, a melody is present for the rest of the day.

It is a beautiful melody that has nothing to do with rolling over in the clover, laying down or doing it again. Ugh, Ugh, Ugh.

Today I am fulfilled. I set the night on fire as I emerge from the cavern, ascend the corridor, pass through the mouth of the cave and onto the threshold of the ledge on a mountain. I take the fresh air of life fully into my lungs.

Suddenly, there is a kerfuffle. A little boy melts down in the hallway. He slams the door, kicks over a little table and begins to rip the drawings of his classmates off the bulletin board. He is pursued by his worker. She is so gentle with him. He turns and tries to kick her, so she holds him to keep him safe. He tries to smash his head into her chin. His rage is that feral. I join in and together we restrain this little Stinky, until his writhing stops, his breathing quiets and he begins to feel sheepish for spitting on us. When he is ready, we stand him up, brush him off and help him pick up the drawings.

I return to the ledge and take a good view of the valley floor. My gaze lifts to the mountain across the tree tops. I am exhausted. Like a nighthawk, I rise, get loft and with a good wind behind me, bank to ascend like an arrow shot on bent wings.

I am alone when I land. Old Gray is nowhere to be found. I did not really expect him. It is Friday night and I could murder a drink.

Chord iii
(the blue tail fly)

"What'll it be, Jimmy?"

"Pour me a smash, no ice and one for my friend, here. Thanks, Sammy."

The Brontosaurus and I spot a quiet table, leave the bar and go have a seat. It is a nice room, done tastefully in off-whites with just a hint of grey on the trim. Group of Seven prints hang at intervals along the walls. The overall effect is tidy and clean.

"Here it is," I say.

One day I go for a walk and when I swing my arms, they are sore at the back, just below my shoulders. It is an odd sensation, different than anything I am used to.

"Did you tell anybody?" the Brontosaurus asks

"The irritation is not enough to do anything about. It just bugs me," I say.

The next week on my walk, I notice the feeling again, only this time, my arms feel heavy, like gravity pulls them down to the centre of the earth.

"Did you see a dinosaur with a sail on its back?"

"*Buh dee chee chee,*" I reply.

It helps when I put my hands in the pockets of my jacket. That seems to take the pressure off. When the pressure is off, I figure it will all go away. Well it does not go away and one night I sit in the chair and I just cannot get comfortable. There is no gravity on my arms, but still, they feel sore.

"So, you tell somebody, now, right?" Brontosaurus asks.

"As a matter of fact, I don't. I figure I have it covered, point man and all that. I am Jimmy the Bleeder, after all."

"More like Jimmy the Arse," she says.

Anyway, I get in the car and take myself to the Civic. It costs me a billion dollars to park. It is not too busy and when they ask me what my issue is, the plot thickens. Do not pass go, go to the head of the line, and all that. My sleeve is up and I hate that rubber band they tie on. Fine if you don't have hair on your arms but I do and nobody gets it right. Pinches like hell.

"And the other Jimmy Crack Corn, eh?"

"Right. You got it. Master's gone away and I don't care. Blue tail fly time. Well, the next thing I know, they are back only it is three of them and they all look serious. Am I sure I am okay and all that, have a seat: I can have some water a little later on. A dozen bees in pink and light blue swarm me. I remember that old Stooge joke from Saturday mornings in *Oncewuz*."

"Do you know what a pippin is? A pippin is an apple with its core on the inside."

"Have you ever-seen-an-apple-with-its-core-on-the-outside?"

"Yes, I have."

"That's a knee-slapper," Brontosaurus says.

"Anyway," I say. "A triglyceride is an enzyme with its arse in my bloodstream and the next thing you know, I do the Roach Motel. The roaches check in … but they don't … check out!"

"Remember, I came to get you three days later?" she says. "I do. It is a snowstorm and you let me drive."

"Sammy, two more please. One for me and the other one for me," I say.

"Jimmy, can you sing 'Over the Hill and Far Away'? Sammy asks.

"Yes, so why don't you!" is the correct response.

We both roar in unison.

Life is filled with recurring themes. All conversations tend to converge. The final call to service is no more noble than the first. In the morning, I take to the air and fly eastward to a portion of the Charred City that is not so desolate. There is not much urban war in it or maybe it is all war and perhaps as a DoGooder, I now find war so normal I no longer notice it. I am never quite sure. From the air, I spy farm fields and row upon row of my sexy green corn. I love the colour of oats. Those fields fairly wave to me from the ground. The sun is on high, behind me and warms my back. The neighbourhoods in the city continue to push back the fields. All buildings have a pre-packaged look, with clean lines and not much graffiti. Even from the sky, I note that none of the variety stores are Ma and Pa operations. Sure, it is still *Neverwuz*, but there is no tenderloin section yet to speak of. The entire region looks like a kid dressed up to go to church. Something is off and the clothes never fit right. Appearances do deceive and there is always something to confess in *Neverwuz*. It is the way it is. In a corner, at the end of a block with wide streets, marquee lights flash. A string of bass clarinet notes hitch their fluid ride on the musical scale that air currents create. They pass clean through me and I, Jimmy the Bleeder, am revitalized. Eric Dolphy has residency here. There is much more jazz in my life now. I am older. My tear ducts still work but I need a change. Change beats burnout is the straight way to tell it.

Somebody likes what I do with dinosaurs and toilet paper. I shake hands and, in the ratio and proportion of cheaper housing, I commute for the next quarter century. In the days before apps, when cassette players walk the earth, I play language tapes in the car. By the end of my first decade, I speak eighteen languages fluently. By the second decade, I am a linguistic master and by the third decade in a twist of fate, I turn into the tower of babel and revert to garbled Martian. I love it in the mornings, when there is time to sip coffee, think and plan my day. In the evenings I just want to get home along with the other half of the planet. Home to supper and hearth and the warmth of rye in the Inn. The money is infinitely better and I get the summers off to play and recoup my losses. It is an odd path from baby snatcher to cave healer to bounty hunter. It is an odd thing to get good at something you never plan to do. The beauty of bounty hunting is that the mission is clear.

In the Charred City there are a million distractions to the universal edict to stay in school. What is so wrong with five days a week, 190 days a year, the push and pull to share, learning and new adults and homework? There are friends in the bargain, teams to join, instruments to play, or maybe not.

If only it were that simple. At what point does my sight change? At what point am I not in spirit form? When do I realize that few objects are fixed in time and space. How can a river have three names? Why did the nighthawk cross the road? To avoid Old Gray's road apples or not-colour Dad's sticky stuff, that's why. My psychosis is applied. It is of my own free will. Perhaps it protects the innocence that is *Oncewuz*. Is innocence the corner stone? What the hell is it about Dug Hill Cemetery anyway? What an ordeal. Too much of a muchness. I hate going back to find something I cannot find; to search for it and weep. Better to bring it along forever so I won't have to go back and look for it again. It makes sense at the time.

Buh dee chee chee.

The questions are like a scent. I wander left, now right, now left, circle like an old hound and get distracted by the mission. The questions are like a haunt that I shiver and forget about. When I forget the questions, I am shit-kicked, thrown into a ditch and then dragged to the Inn.

"Sammy? Pour this DoGooder a double shot! Put a roof over his head, check his wounds and send him out tomorrow," I hear a Samaritan say.

I see a lot of Rosellas in my new world. I am amazed in a large system to find hundreds of little Stinky's in the hallway; while teachers and teams make do, accommodate, strategize and put their finger in the dike. To a Stinky, each of these bruised boys and girls are similar to the children the six dinosaurs helped before I came here. I know how to help them. It is the experience and not the education. After school I meet a beautiful little girl who does not speak anymore. Her parents swear that she was fine right up until she got a vaccine. Not many others believe them but they are sure they know. At the conference, I count twelve "helpers." Each has a specialty. When I go out to help these parents connect with the school (and vice versa), somehow in their schedule they find time for me. I am honoured. I confess to them that I am not important in the grand arc of things past, things present and things yet to come. For the rest of the spring, we have tea and long talks. There is no magic to it other than I am the only Soul who comes to them, noting parking is a bitch. Like me, they never know if the barrier is actually going to lift when they put their credit card in the machine at the hospital.

It takes me a month of tracking to locate two teenagers and their father. The boys are not in school. When they do attend, I hear they are respectful. Their only problem is that they live in a van. I am struck by their sense of humour and how close as brothers they are. To see love and loyalty in that close is a gift. I am not sure why another young person uses abortion as a birth-control method. She does okay at school when she shows up. There is a naivete about her that lets people in so that all of us, me, the nurse, a teacher and three other souls, become a kind of composite family to help her graduate. She graduates. Against all odds, so many of them do. Some are so angry they are immobilized. They cannot attend class and they can not drop out. They look like wolves in silhouette, head down, lurking, always on the edge, wild and mistrustful. I send word through a tame wolf that I wish to meet with them. A couple of them send word back to invite me to fuck right off, but a pack of them agree. I know I am older than them, decrepit some might say, but the humiliation of Rosella's eyes in a hallway is universal. Gently, we get as many off the margin as we can. Some return to class and some need help to just get the fuck out and go to work. Some are not ready to do a thing. Some want to get off the radar, so they can return to the business of dealing drugs. Leopard-skin papers never fade away. They just smell funny. I meet a thousand young spirits, alone, separated from their countries, away from their friends, away from any sense of connectedness. There is no smell of home. They live in nice apartments and are here to get a better education if they don't die from depression first. There is no back-up plan. Out of necessity, we get good at heading razor blades, Tylenol and brown nooses off at the pass. En route, I become a kind of social journalist. A colleague and I collect the best and brightest ideas from every high school in the district on how to help young people not end it. I have no idea where I learn to do this. The politics are heavy. The farther an administrator is away from the front line, the more problematic it is to admit that kids try to hurt themselves. It is bad theatre. The front line craves the wisdom, so we go rogue and share what we learn. A beautiful girl is seduced into the underground current of human sex trafficking. Her classroom is a hotel. There is no way math cuts it anymore. No more red stars for excellent work. I see innocence so deep down, it no longer emerges from its protected cavern in the heart. It is captive. Involuntarily held against its will. It is hard to be in spirit form and willfully enter that cavern and be turned back. To see innocence behind bars, smiling. To not have the skill to help. To be rendered powerless. To feel useless. To be beaten by a power greater than my own. Maybe the cops will do a better job. I hear the echo of innocence on the cynical edge of laughter. I see it in a glint of tear, no bigger than a pin-prick. Innocence looks like the tail-fin goodbye of a carp, as it disappears upriver into the murk of the FishnShit. It is in the dial tone of a hung-up phone. Perhaps it is mixed into a small square of marble. How should I know?

In the days before apps, when DoGooders roam the earth, it really is bounty hunting. To venture out, find, coax and coerce and bring back alive. That is the mission. Tag 'em and bag 'em. To offer a reality other than the Charred City. Once I was chastised for it.

"Jimmy, you arse! What did you bring her back for? She misses too many days, it is late in the semester and there is nothing we can do for her."

"Well, the Other Jimmy Crack Corn," I say. "If you don't know what to do, do something."

And so on.

Around the time my hearing begins to fail, I get promoted to Band Leader. By now I am fluent in seven languages: Twi, Tagolog, Mandarin, English, Polish, Edu-speak and DoGooder-ese. Nobody hears a word I say, until the drummer tells me: "Jimmy. Do not be afraid to lead. We all need to be led."

So, I buckle down, strap on the bass clarinet and get the band to play in tune. Each one is a gifted soloist. We play night after night to sold-out audiences. It is a small stage but our reach is enormous. Marquis lights blink far into the night and the bar is packed on the outskirts of the Charred City. It is my band and we have a certain residency. Composition after composition, chord after chord, appear out of nowhere, like a nighthawk's flash through lamp lights on a street of gold. It stuns me. Tonight, we woodshop a BeBop tune called "*Lamprocapnos Spectabilis.*" "Lampro Spectis" for short. The band and I are in the pocket, all night.

In the morning, full circle: I find myself at a conference table deep in the Charred City. I am asked to be a part of baby snatcher group called Death Review. We try to understand and draw lessons from children who are immolated or die by accident in the care of those who have a little orange card with no picture on it; only by now, they have pictures on their cards. It is sacred work and has the unintended effect of purging most of my demons. I have no idea why. I have no idea why I am so fond of this particular band of DoGooders whose sole mission is to protect and preserve the innocence in all of us. Thankfully, I am not asked to do this every morning. Two years, two months, two days and there but for the grace of Jimmy Crack Corn, go I ... is the crazy way to tell it again. Stories must be repeated to make life right.

When I get home, there is a letter from Pinky in the mailbox. I don't have time to open it. I do have time to shower and then get down to the Marquee for a sound check.

The set goes well but my arms grow tired by the gravity of holding up my instrument. The band and I rework a cover of Link Wray's *Black Widow*, only we do it in an alternating 9/8ths, 4/4 time. I do not know where I learn to play like this. The sound soars and I realize I have come of age. Perhaps my journey is done. Improvisation will do that. There is some fright to finishing a good tune. The other side of getting good at something I did not set out to do, is to have the time to do something with no idea how to spend it. I listen for the clip-clop of Old Gray but I am on my own now. Like I say, call me Icarus.

During a break in the set, I sit at the bar and talk to Sammy.

"I'll have what ever it is I'm having," I tell him, over the din of tinkling glass and chatter.

"Oh. You mean a double? Why didn't you say so?" Sammy replies.

"*Buh dee chee chee*," I tell him.

"Sammy? I get this letter from my friend Pinky. He is out in the oil patch and makes a good life. We lose touch for a while. Pinky's one claim to fame is that in his entire career he never gets laid off. That's big in the oil business. When he retires, the HR people think he knows the drill and are flabbergasted he does not. I think it is because he organizes a ball hockey league for any employee who wants to play. Thirty years in a row. He rents the gym, collects the money, organizes the roster, buys the markers and records the round-robin. The man is gold in his organization. I come from *Oncewuz*, and we play road hockey every night after school over on Joel-the-Hole's street. Pinky's people are gamers. We go back to his place after hockey and the Old Boy and Old Girl play bridge. The radio is in the bottom of the sixth. Their television gets a first down. There are clubs, diamonds, spades and hearts on the highball glasses. It is like that with them.

"Anyway, Sammy, I open this thick letter and there are twelve blank pages and one self-addressed stamped envelope. Get this. The letter starts with *'Dear Pinky, it has been a while since I wrote you ...'* and then ends with *'Your devoted Arse of a friend, Jimmy the Bleeder.'*"

"That is one hell of a pal," Sammy says as he mops down the bar. "What do you do?"

"Geezis, what do you think I do? I sit down and write him a thirteen-page letter, just so that Ape knows I exceed his expectation." I tell Sammy.

"Not many guys will do that, Jimmy. At the end of the day, there are not many friends who will do an all-out search to find you. You should listen to a guy like that. Ashes to ashes, dust to dust. If Rotz don't get ya, Nettle must. Break whatever trance you are in and get your priorities straight, Bub."

"Who dies and turns you into a DoGooder?" I ask Sammy but he disappears on me.

I am outside now. The air is damp and fresh. The streetlights are on and somehow, I find myself home.

On the morning of the millionth day in the Charred City, my feet touch the ground and I am on a farm. I peel the wax off my wings. All the feathers are there and I am in one piece. The Marquee lights are gone and all I have to show for it is a purple heart and a combat medal. I take a deep pull of air into my lungs and despite all the cigarettes, they expand like they are supposed to. I feel my rib cage and my breast swell with a certain pride. Cherubims pay the Innkeeper and leave me, with no fanfare.

My farm is somewhere in the north, in a suburb, and all the houses look the same. Aluminum siding replaces the asbestos shingles and it is not unpleasant. The driveway slopes down and pulls up in front of the garage. It is a bitch to shovel snow in the winter. My tomatoes grow along the side in the full sun and there is rhubarb in the back. It is a good year for tomatoes but as my neighbours say, the season is not over yet. I pinch off the suckers, keep the weeds down and cultivate the soil. There is a silo in the back and everyone repeats the country joke that that is where us farmers stash our money. In my mind, I see row after row of my sexy green corn. It pushes through the soil right on time. Knee high by July and all that hubbub.

Across the road next to me, a schoolyard is in full throttle. There are screams of abject glee and in the pandemonium, boys shoot cards up against the brick wall by the dodgeball tether. Gaggle upon gaggle of girls talk by the swings and everybody is decent and takes their turn. The adults stand around in clusters of two. They quietly watch the romp and folly and for all the world look like beautiful sheepdogs guarding a fold. I stop to hear the happy screeching. To me it all sounds the way wildflowers smell. My eyes focus and four girls chose sides for the next game.

Ocha bocca, donna crocka
Occca bocca diss,
Cin-der-ella, um-bar-ella
Out goes Miss!

One girl stands dutifully by the side and waits to be united with her partner. Repeat to infinity. There is perhaps, nothing more beautiful to watch.

There is a small barn in the back yard, where I keep my tools. In the season of harvest, I have everything by now; dandelion spears, leaf rakes, a hickory broom, hoes and cultivators, a good steel pry bar to loan the neighbours and then wonder where I left it. My eyes rest upon an edger. Half crescent, painted green with a short sturdy stock and a handle with a good grip. There is a trowel in a balsa basket next to it and beside that, leaning against the inner wall, an old willow shovel that was my father's. I tend to keep everything and that is a blessing and a burden according to my Brontosaurus. There are cracks and ridges along the length of the shovel. When I touch it, I smell wet bark, hear the creak of nautical rope and hurl off into a small oblivion of memory, to drop, steel-straight, into the River of Joy. Behind the little barn, a tiny garden opens to the full sun. It is bordered by beautiful rocks that my Stegosaurus and I pick along the way or drag back from a cottage, somewhere long ago. White and red rosy quartz: obsidian that always looks wet and living somehow. Two plastic hens in laying form sprout geraniums out of their backs. They peck and squabble and when I look at them, I am more in love. It is here, as a joke, I plant a row of five *Lamprocapnos* plants—"bleeding hearts," some call them. It is spring and they flower. The flower-heads, heart-shaped and bulbous, droop downwards, rich, fulsome and made heavy by the sexiness of gravity. Each one drips a little white off its tip, like a tear. The effect is far from sorrow; in fact, the plants make me laugh and when I laugh, I remember. Of course, I give them all names and one of them is named Fizzy.

"*Buh dee chee chee*, you old Arse," I hear myself say.

By now school is well over and the street is stilled by an odd quiet. The sun has left her glorious Technicolor. There are extended spaces between the chords. Rose-colour swirls behind the clouds, define their fluffy edges, in a darker shade of blue. It is soon time for nighthawks. I have twenty minutes or so before the street lamps come on. Stupid June bugs drape off everything. For a while I feel them in my hair and do the palsy dance to get them the hell off my neck and arms. All bees leave for the night. They are so busy today. Their legs dangle and puff with weight, like yellow saddlebags.

There is a game we play in the water, with a football and I think of that just now.

We call it *Gipper Death-Ball*. Stand fifteen feet apart. Chest deep in the brine. Throw the ball as hard as you can at your opponent. One-skip it off the surface and when it skips, it accelerates. If you catch it, good. Skip it back, like a rocket at your opponent. If she misses it altogether, that is called an ace. An ace is worth two points. A headshot is worth three. If she fails to make the catch altogether and the football bobs on the water, we call that a muff: point for you, game to eleven, thirteen to break a tie. Repeat to infinity. When it is time to leave, go directly to the roadside stand, for French fries and grease. Smother everything in malt vinegar and salt.

The air is laden with moisture now in ratio and proportion to the waning light. I know I must hurry or be haunted forever. I begin to hum.

Jimmy Crack Corn and I don't care.

I go to the barn and gather up the edger and the trowel. I walk around back, by the bleeding hearts. I measure with my eyes and find a spot near Fizzy. The grass is thick and rich here. I step on the edger with the ball of my foot and puncture the soil when the blade slips in. I do that three more times and form a perfect 8-by-8-inch square. I go down on my knees to smell the fullness of the earth. I place my finger along the edges to pull back and widen the gap. Slowly, I peel the grass away. The green thatch hesitates at first and then tears away like a scalp.

Jimmy Crack Corn and I don't care.

I take the trowel and plunge it in, to loosen the soil for depth. I scrape it out and continue to scrape until I am a foot down. I pile the excess soil in a little mound and if anyone sees me, I am sure they see that my actions are efficient.

There is a plastic grocery bag next to my knee. I peel it back and remove its contents. So much time passes, I forget how heavy it is. The letters are clean and there is no mud.

In the hollow, I carefully place my two medals. I cup both hands to pull the dirt into the hole. When everything is completely covered, I pat it tenderly with the palm of my hand and press the thatch of grass on top. I stand now, stretch, look around and I have no idea what to do. If I do anything tomorrow, I know I need to find my dinosaurs and play is the tired way to tell it.

My master's gone a-way.

Afterword

Jimmy Crack Corn: A Novel in C Minor is a story from the heart and soul. The author was influenced by the interior spiritual meaning(s) of the ancient "field song," "Jimmy Crack Corn." The melody's rhythm, intent, cadence and chorus weave throughout the tale. Perhaps the story is made stronger by the gifts of curious possibility suggested within the lyrics. An interested reader may find clues by carrying out a simple online search for this poignant song, so filled with projective meaning in the animate spaces of living between chordal moments in time.